What readers are sayir

"*The Naked Storytelle*
of fiction."

"It's funny!"

"Almost spit my coffee out."

"It is a very easy read—despite the quite serious issues involved—because Thomas writes so well."

"Thomas delivers some serious food for thought about choosing your own path in life, the role of technology in modern society and even a middle-aged romance, all rolled up into one hilarious package."

"To write about storytelling puts a certain amount of pressure on the author to deliver something special, and Thomas and her story do not disappoint."

"I understand where this book is coming from and found it very relatable."

"It will be a best seller. I can feel it in my bones."

Books by Laura Michelle Thomas

The Naked Storyteller

Polly Wants to Be a Writer:
The Junior Authors Guide to Writing and Getting Published

THE NAKED STORYTELLER

BY
LAURA MICHELLE THOMAS

Produced by:

 **FriesenPress**

Suite 300 – 852 Fort Street
Victoria, BC, Canada V8W 1H8
www.friesenpress.com

ISBN
978-1-4602-4619-1 (Hardcover)
978-1-4602-4620-7 (Paperback)
978-1-4602-4621-4 (eBook)

1. Fiction, Humorous

Distributed to the trade by The Ingram Book Company

For Alan

THE NAKED STORYTELLER

PART ONE

1

I was such a coward the day I first saw her. I was. That's the naked truth.

It was raining, nothing newsworthy for Vancouver in February. I stood under the grimy plexiglass entryway of Sundry Tech, the biggest and most modern high school in the district, deliberating whether or not I should be a good boy and go to class. It was February 14, a Friday, and the first professional day of the new year. A professional day, another waste-of-my-time professional day. I was sick of teaching, permanently nauseous. The education system was under my skin like an infection; my students were hives. I had let the conference brochure sit in my mailbox in the school office until the week before the conference, when we all got an ugly email from the head of our local branch of the Alliance of Teachers reminding us conference attendance was mandatory, and that we shouldn't treat a professional development day like a hall pass. I took the brochure home for the weekend but didn't look at it. It was James—my friend and a young-but-okay fellow grade-six teacher at Dugwood Elementary—who suggested I let fate choose my workshops. The idea sounded dumb enough to fit with the theme of education in general. So, the night of the final registration deadline, I cleared the empty cereal boxes and potato chip bags off my kitchen table; I rummaged around in a utensil drawer I never knew existed and found a metal barbecue skewer; I opened the conference brochure to the middle page, closed my eyes and chose two workshops. I ended up with Surviving the Picket Line in the morning and How to Maximize Your Pension Income in the afternoon. The deed done, I stuffed the brochure in the pocket of my trench coat, buttoned up my sweater vest, and grit through the four-day week by the skin of my raw nerves.

Now I stood outside Sundry's front doors in my damp trench coat, buttoned-up sweater vest and ill-fitting jeans, like an idiot, as the other late-risers, heel-draggers and tardy delinquents rushed by, clutching their totes and shaking their wet umbrellas at me. As far as I was concerned I was under attack. I took everything so personally back then; such a coward I was standing there in my size fourteens. I had four and a half months until my annual summer firing, and I was sure I would be worn down to a nub by June. In twenty-five years of teaching grade six I had the worst class.

For years, I had been witnessing the gradual decline of self-respect, manners and self-care. But that year—the year I met *her*—my students were the absolute rock-bottom, make-you-want-to-drink bunch of self-centred bullies I had ever been incarcerated with. Every morning after the announcements, I had to restrain myself from kicking them all out. Let Mommy and Daddy deal with the little dunces in their spare minutes between work and chauffeuring their little princes and princesses to their activities. No matter what generation you are talking about, nearly-pubescent kids are a pain; that's their job. I was too; I get that. But, nowadays, with all this being treated like "the chosen one," kids are getting measurably stupider. I swear on the grave of my recently-departed mother, Adelle Tyke, they are. Kids do not say please and thank you. They screech when they don't get their way. They can't wait two minutes for something they want without freaking out. They threaten to hit you over the head with their tablets when you ask them to turn off their games and come to class. They cannot walk themselves to and from school, and when they do walk they don't watch where they are going. They certainly never say excuse me if they bump into you. And basic oral hygiene, such as brushing twice a day, that little nugget of wisdom has fallen by the wayside somehow too.

Many of my students that year had such bad breath I could actually feel the hairs in my nose curl tighter and pierce the insides of my nostrils when they got too close to me. I figure that evenings in their households went something like this: "Bed time," says the parent, without looking up from the computer. "No!" shrieks the child. This goes back and forth until the child falsely capitulates. "Did you brush your teeth?" asks the parent, still at the computer. "Yes," lies the child, who then takes the tablet to his or her bedroom and plays until he or she passes out. That's why at the start of the school year I rearranged my classroom so that the students could only get within a desk-length of me when handing in their assignments. And when I was on my feet, I kept moving; I made sure I never stood still longer than I could comfortably breathe through my mouth. The fact they cannot seem to be taught to brush and floss daily is testament to the deepening stupidity I am talking about. What a class! With the number of times I had thought about quitting, it must have been fate or fear or plain laziness that kept me teaching that winter. Looking back, it was probably all three rolled into a hairy, middle-aged mess.

My class was almost equally split, gender-wise. The girls had a brutal hierarchy in which there were insiders and definite outsiders, who were ruled over by an indomitable alpha group that liked to pick on me about my clothes and beard. With bold disrespect, they called me Beast. And though I am a fairly large, fairly hairy man, I did not like it. Worse, it bothered me that their remarks bothered me. At fifty-two, I was supposed to be tougher than that. Wasn't I?

The twelve boys in my class were what my grandfather would have called "yard apes," though the term didn't apply perfectly since their yard was a video screen, not an outdoor one made of grass and dirt and rocks and things. Nonetheless, there was something wrong with their brains, both individually and collectively. Those boys actually seemed to be hardwired to ignore and refuse anything I said; they were defiant to the marrow. I have always wondered if the unlimited video gaming of their early years had damaged the politeness and respect centres in their brains. And, unlike a decade ago, it wasn't just the students with behaviour labels who were especially difficult; it was all of them, every last boy. It was like they had been meticulously designed to blossom into self-centred, manipulative, gimme-everything-now-or-I-will-rant adults. It is such a strange way to raise children. Truly strange.

It was getting late, and I was still standing outside the school doors working up the nerve to leave. I wanted so badly to be a bad boy (not a yard ape, but a true heroic bad boy). I pulled the damp conference brochure out of my trench coat pocket and looked up my first workshop: Surviving the Picket Line with Gretta Hagride.

Join teacher and former AOBCT shop steward Gretta Hagride for a two-hour workshop that will get you ready for the next walkout. Ms. Hagride will discuss tips from her self-published book, Surviving the Picket Line, which will be available from the author at the end of the workshop for a $25 donation to the One Laptop Per Child initiative.

Surviving the Picket Line, I vowed to never read it but was instantly jealous of Ms. Hagride. I had always wanted to write, not mundane how-to manuals like hers but rocking-good fiction with outrageous heroes, insanely enticing heroines and villains that made your nose hairs curl.

I saw through the glass front doors that I had already missed the keynote on digital teaching resources with a Dr. So-and-so. The foyer and nearby cafeteria were rapidly filling with my colleagues—one or two smiling and chatting excitedly, some looking for a caffeine fix, others on their way to the toilet or to have a smoke before the workshops started. I debated whether or not I had the courage to ditch the whole thing, give myself a well-earned hall pass, and go to Jitters for a coffee and a good read. I loved a good novel and liked the Jitters vibe enough that every Saturday, from nine until noon, I would sit at my favourite table near the back of the Jitters in my neighbourhood, sipping their house blend while reading from a real paper book—not from a tablet or mega cell phone. There was something about the slightly oily touch and inky smell of a book that turned me on. I also liked the fact that on the average Saturday morning between nine and noon there were very few children. There were lots of polite, male urbanites with designer glasses and brown berets or black fedoras, several attractive women with scarves wrapped dashingly around their elegant necks, fashionable middle-aged cyclists and runners who came in sweaty and thirsty after their morning jaunt, but rarely any children.

I made up my mind: I wasn't going to the conference. I was going to skip out, go to Jitters, drink good coffee, and read. So, with a lie fixed in my brain—I was coming down with the flu—and with my head down and trench coat collar up, I took one step away from Sundry and ploughed into someone who, at that exact moment, was rushing towards the front doors.

A bright yellow tool box fell on the cement and broke open. A brass candlestick clanged on the concrete, and a white candle rolled into the dirt under the shrubbery.

"Excuse me," said a woman, who was now crouched down and picking up her things.

I shuffled out of her way, head down, beard pressed into my neck to avoid having to talk to her. I took two steps away and stopped. That teenage, wannabe-writer, romantic part of me that still believed in rescuing distressed damsels wanted to help her. So I turned around, squatted next to her and leaned into the shrubbery. I fished out one of the candles, brushed the wet soil off and handed it to her. We both stood up.

"Thank you." She smiled and looked up at me. Her teeth were perfectly white, whiter than the candle I had just handed her. Stunning.

She tried to pull the candle out of my hand. I didn't let go nor did I speak.

"Thank you," she repeated, tugging at the candle.

After a moment I let go. Then, wanting to continue as the gentleman-hero, I flung one of my gigantic arms out to open the door for her, but I misjudged the distance and smashed my pinky finger against the metal door handle.

"Ouch... stupid, sorry," were the first words I mumbled to her.

She smiled at me as she stepped around my gut and squeezed inside. I stood there completely blocking the doorway, watching her walk away from me across the foyer. I didn't like that she was walking away from me. She wore tights and had her bare feet inside candy-red high heels; her shoes were glossy red like a fashion model's shiny lipstick. Her stride was unlike any stride I had ever seen on a teacher. A strange, sweetish sensation was coming over me.

"Are you going in or out?" said an agitated young man who was trying to get inside. "You're blocking the door!"

"Sorry," I mumbled, letting go of the handle and stepping inside the cavernous entryway. A sign painted on the wall to the right of the doors said in two-foot high, blue script: *Be the author of your own life.* But I didn't notice the sign, not that day. I was too stunned, watching the woman with the red heels, who was getting her conference package from the sweatshirt-clad ladies at the registration table. I watched her, stared at her, until a handful of Dugwood teachers walked across my view. I could see they were pretending not to notice me. They pretended because they didn't want to have to come up and say hello to Harry Tyke. I wasn't on good terms with any of the teacher cliques at our school.

The young, optimistic, trendy set thought I was ridiculous. The older and crustier ones, like me, were jaded and kept more to themselves, like I did. The ones in the middle could take or leave me. For years, I had been going out to my car to eat lunch. I couldn't stand the staffroom, and the staff couldn't stand me, except for young James who had only been at Dugwood for two years. He seemed to get a kick out me, and I didn't mind his energy and youthful confidence.

Now that I had both my size fourteens inside the high school, I was officially going to the conference. I was such a weenie. I still could have left and told everyone on Monday that I had come down with a sudden case of stomach flu, and no one would have questioned it. But I didn't leave. I didn't have the courage and, besides, something about watching the woman in the red high heels had caused a strange sensation to flow through me. I felt warm and a little lightheaded. I felt very strange, especially in the mid-section, plus my throat was tight and sticky. It was like walking through Chinatown and being hit with the sweet smells of the herb shops and exotic fruit stands. I suddenly noticed something: the shirt underneath my sweater vest was strained to bursting and a racoon-sized roll of fat was threatening to slide over my belt. The roll of fat and my tight shirt bothered me. Maybe I really was sick and should just head home. For some reason though, despite having a perfectly reasonable excuse for skipping the conference, I dismissed the strange feeling, chalking it up to ongoing malaise, despicable students and low caffeine levels. I unbuttoned my trench coat and went to get myself a free coffee.

At the cream and sugar table, I received a swift, unwarranted jolt in the lower back, which made me slop coffee on my sweater vest. I blamed James, thin and neatly dressed in black except for bright orange sneakers, who had just reached across my personal space for a plastic lid to put on his paper coffee cup.

"It wasn't me," James whispered. "It was her and she's..." He licked his lips.

I didn't look. Why should I care about some woman who had just invaded my personal space? I had been staunchly single since my divorce so I was not interested in ogling some woman who had just elbowed me in the lower back. I was irritated not interested. I put a lid on my coffee cup, turned to James and asked him what workshop he was going to.

James was still staring at the woman standing behind me. He took a sip of coffee and said quietly, "How do you ask a teacher out on a date?"

"That's a workshop?" I sputtered. A dribble of coffee had rolled down the wrong pipe. ·

"No, you idiot, how do I ask that teacher out on a date?"

"What teacher?"

"The one who helped you spill coffee on yourself." James lifted his soft chin to indicate who he was talking about.

I turned to look. It was her, the woman with the red high heels. She was hustling away from me again, this time with a large coffee in hand. I felt too warm in my sweater vest and that sweet, sticky sensation was building again. I put my coffee down and used the two sides of my trench coat to fan myself.

"By the time you're scarfing down your chicken wrap," said James, "I will have a date with her."

"No, you won't," I blurted out with more ferocity than I had intended. I stopped fanning myself, and told myself to reign "it" in, though I was unsure what "it" was. I said with more calm in my voice, "You're not going to ask a woman like that out for a first date on Valentine's Day. It's too cliché—desperate! Besides, a woman like that is not single. It's not possible."

"I already know her name." James smiled and pointed his rolled up conference brochure at the hallway through which the woman had disappeared. "She is Olga and she is gorgeous and—" He stopped speaking and gave me a good long look. "What's wrong with you this morning, Beast? You're more worked up than usual." He jammed some napkins into my hand. "Would you wipe the coffee off that hideous vest. Don't you ever buy new clothes?"

I took the wad of napkins, shoved them in the still-damp pocket of my trench coat and picked up my coffee. "There's nothing wrong with my clothes."

"That's one way to spin it when you're old and decrepit—but, listen, why can't I get a woman like that to go out with me? I think it's perfect that it's Valentine's Day. Did you see her legs and those heels? Wow! If she's single she'll jump at the chance to go out with me. No woman wants to be alone on Valentine's Day. Not a woman who wears shoes like that."

"Now who's spinning tales? You're not in her league." I took a sip of coffee and wondered if that was true. I knew I wasn't in her league, and maybe she was into younger, skinnier, less-hairy men. The thought annoyed me immensely.

"No wonder your students call you Beast."

"Shut up," I said, rubbing the long, greying whiskers on my cheeks and chin.

"When was the last time you looked at yourself in the mirror? Have you thought about trimming that thing, at least trying to make it look like a style?"

I smoothed my beard with my free hand. "I did, yesterday."

James lifted his glasses off his nose to inspect my face. "Well, Beast, it's irrelevant whether or not you think I'm in her league. I'm asking her out after her workshop," he paused, "...unless it's boring. I don't date boring women, even when they look like that."

I was just about to take a sip but I stopped my coffee midair and asked, "What do you mean *her* workshop?"

"She is—she was—a teacher in our district about ten years ago. Now she does storytelling workshops and performs at libraries and schools. She spent time in Mexico teaching kids with nothing, literally nothing, no supplies, not even books or a whiteboard—literally nothing."

"That's impossible."

"According to her bio in the brochure, she was in a village that was decimated by a drug turf war and there was nothing left of the school, just empty cinderblock rooms, not a book or pencil, no teaching supplies. I heard that during her last year a bunch of supplies—including laptops and one of those Internet-connected whiteboards—were sent down to her from the States. But, by then, the students were so used to learning through stories that they weren't keen on all the technological gadgets that our students love. Plus they—"

"Fell in love with her," I said, swallowing hard.

James looked at me like I had just asked him out on a date and was about to say something, but I kept talking.

"I mean…you know what I mean. They liked it. Little kids love that stuff, but just primaries, right? If we started telling stories in Health and Career about how we screwed up our marriages and took jobs that we hate to pay off fancy houses we never wanted—"

James held up his hand. "I don't know about failed marriages and debt, but whatever. Who cares about storytelling! I totally agree with you. It's for primary teachers. I'm going to her workshop because she's hot. That's it."

I held out my hand. "Ten bucks she'll turn you down."

James took it. "Ten bucks says she won't."

We shook on it.

James asked, "Did I show you the title of her workshop?"

I laughed. "Don't bother trying to talk me into going with you." I said the words, but I didn't really mean them. I wanted desperately to go to this woman's workshop. I didn't care what it was called.

James unrolled his conference brochure, flipped to the last page and handed it to me. I looked at Olga's photo. It was her, and she was hot, and I could understand why James had signed up. And there was the workshop title: The Naked Storyteller.

"Yeah," said James, his mouth open slightly, revealing a track of clear braces over what looked to me like perfectly straight teeth, "The Naked Storyteller."

I handed James his brochure, threw my half-drunk, non-Jitters coffee in a nearby trash bin and said, "I'm in. Let's go."

"What did you originally sign up for?" asked James as he followed me.

"The one about strikes." A moment later I added, "I hope her workshop isn't full."

James looked at me. "Don't get any ideas, Beast. I've got first dibs."

"Unless it's boring."

"Right. Unless it's boring. I don't do boring women. But something tells me she's not going to be boring," he said, grinning.

I ignored him, and his grin, and walked as quickly as I could without breaking into a jog, with James right on my heels all the way there. When we found the classroom—it was the drama room—we found a pile of shoes in the hallway and a sign on the door that said: *No late entries, please.* I peered through the narrow window that ran the length of the closed door. There was a large group sitting in chairs in a circle. The lights were off, and the white candle I had rescued from the dirt now burned in the brass candlestick, which sat on the carpeted floor in the middle of the sock-footed participants.

"So much for that," James whispered. "Do you want to hit Jitters for a real cup of coffee?"

I was not in the mood to give up so easily. I had made it this far and the most beautiful woman in the world was on the other side of one little classroom door. I jiggled the knob. It was locked. I was about to knock, but James grabbed my hand away.

"I'm not walking in late," he said. "It's too weird. It looks like they're having a séance."

I pulled my hand free and knocked loudly. The workshop participants turned to look at the door. Olga got up and was crossing the room in bare feet.

"Great," said James. "Way to go, Beast. We look like idiots."

"Nothing new there," I said, cupping my hands around my eyes and peering in through the window so that I could watch Olga. I didn't want to miss a step. She was walking towards me now; I liked that.

The door opened and she smiled at us both which irritated me because I wanted her perfect, white smile for myself. "Leave your shoes here," she said softly, "and put your jackets and belongings down somewhere and come join the circle." Then she spoke to me, just me. "You only need your lovely self, no vest or coat, just you."

I took the opportunity to lean in and whisper, "I'm not signed up."

"That's okay," she whispered back. "If you found your way here, you're meant to be here."

Grinning secretly beneath my beard, I kicked off my running shoes and was horrified to see three big holes in the toes of my socks. I wished silently for two things as I followed Olga into the darkened room: one, that she didn't look down and, two, that my feet didn't smell.

As we approached the circle of about forty people (which consisted of more male intermediate-grade teachers than was typical at a storytelling workshop) she stopped and motioned to me that I should take off my coat and leave my things on a table. Then she left me to strip down and walked over to the circle to take her seat. I immediately noticed there were only two other vacant chairs in the circle—one was as far away from Olga as possible, while the other was right next to hers. By the time I had taken off my trench coat and unbuttoned my vest, James had beaten me to the seat next to hers. Royally annoyed, I walked through the middle of the circle, passing so close to the candle that—James told me later—I almost lit my pants on fire.

2

I confess that I did end up playing the sick card after Olga's workshop and skipped out of the afternoon session. I had really enjoyed her workshop and was genuinely inspired by what she taught us, but it had been a kick in the guts watching James smoothly accept that slip of paper with Olga's phone number on it. I went home immediately, without saying goodbye to James, or thank you to Olga, or stopping at the cafeteria to pick up my free chicken wrap and giant cookie. I then spent the rest of the afternoon moping around my house, trying not to think about it being Valentine's Day. But as evening came on, and the rain subsided and the moon came out, I sat down in my office and decided that I was going to tell my students a story from my life. Bruised ego aside, the simplicity of teaching through story appealed to me, deeply. It was so anti-digital, so practical, so human.

By ten o'clock that night, I had figured out which story to tell. By eleven, I was trying to figure out which parts of the curriculum I could give myself credit for. I wondered: could I get credit for prescribed learning outcomes in "purposeful listening" or "oral language" in Language Arts, or for "judgments and decision making" in Heath and Career, or for "probability" in Math? Which one was the best fit? I eventually decided that my story touched on each of those topics enough that I would give myself credit for all of them. At midnight, it was time to get my story out of my memory and onto my inner "movie screen"—that's what Olga had called the imagination—so I could verbalize it for the students. I was supposed to just see the story in my mind and tell it, without rehearsing, without memorizing. I told it to myself once, out loud while sitting at my desk, then decided to call it a night.

Unable to sleep because I kept imagining James and Olga together, I got up just after two and practiced telling my story. I walked around my bedroom in the dark, telling it out loud to the curtains. Then I went downstairs to the living room—the place where I had signed my life away all those years ago—and told it to the cuckoo clock that my father, a high-flying pilot with Great White North Airlines, had bought for my mother on a layover in Zurich.

James called me the next morning really early like he had been up all night. I answered on the first ring. He told me that his date had been "pretty good" and that I owed him ten dollars. I clenched my fist around the phone as I listened to his nonchalant description of what for me would have been a magical evening. We talked about my story, but my large, thick fingers hit a couple of the number keys on the phone by accident, annoying James. He said he would meet me at Jitters so that I could tell him my story and give him his ten bucks.

When we first sat down at the coffee shop I had that queer, sweetish sensation in my gut and throat again. I had to drink two cups of black, unsweetened coffee to suppress it. I was thankful that James didn't say anything about his date with Olga as we took turns glancing at each other over our respective reading materials. Finally, he interrupted the disjointed non-conversation and told me to get on with my story.

This is what I told him:

"It was the Sunday of Labour Day weekend. I was twenty years old and still living at home with my parents in our big house in Kerrisdale. I was working as a part-time junior copy editor at our local community newspaper for seven and a half dollars an hour. I was keen on being a novelist and spent all my free time reading, watching movies and writing down my story ideas. After dinner, my parents told me they were moving to New Mexico at the end of the month. They were selling the house and wanted to sell it to me but only if they knew I was going to have a good job with a government pension. I explained that I was determined to move my way up the ladder at the newspaper and eventually earn my living as a novelist. My father said that was a lark. They wanted me to get serious, go to university and become a teacher. Being a teacher, they had apparently concluded, would not only be a good fit for me, it would also guarantee me a government pension, plus the security I needed to take over the mortgage payments and, eventually, be the owner of a really nice house in one of the nicest parts of Vancouver. I knew that with interest rates at an all-time high of over twenty percent that I would never find a better deal than what my parents were offering me on their house. But I hated school and was never keen on teaching or teachers and did not agree with my parents that this was the right career for me. I predicted correctly that I would spend the next thirty years of my life being very unhappy in a very nice house that I never really wanted in the first place. But they won, and, that night, I signed a contract to take over the mortgage. A month later, I kissed my mother goodbye at the airport and got into university on a mature student pass. My ex-wife, Cindy, was in the same program. She moved in after we'd been dating a week. She didn't have any money and thought it wasn't fair that I had such a big, fancy house in Kerrisdale all to myself. We got married the year we started teaching; that was in 1987. Then, after twenty-two years together, she left me for this gargantuan guy from Chicago, a high-level video gamer that she had, I found out later, been having an online relationship with for the last few years of our marriage. The end."

I sat back in my chair and looked at James. "Well?"

"Harsh," said James, sipping his coffee.

"I know. But I want these kids to learn five things." I held up my fingers as I counted them out. "One, life is hard—impossible mostly. Two, every decision matters. Three, most of them won't have the courage to follow their dreams. Four, of those who follow their dreams, they can be sure that someone or something will come along and try to derail them. Five, we are mostly miserable."

James shook his head. "You're crazy. Kids eleven and twelve years old don't know what a mortgage is and they don't care." James paused to smile at a pretty barista who was clearing the table next to ours. "Listen, your students are not going to get it and they're not supposed to get it, not yet. You might as well hand them your gonads on a platter." He laughed. "You'll never make it to the end of June."

James was right and wrong. I stared at his braces and wondered why Olga had gone out with him.

When I didn't respond to his comments, he said, "Did you hear that the Education Agency wants to put a freeze on hiring new teachers? They've got some big deal they've signed with an American tech company but they haven't announced it yet." James flipped the newspaper open to a picture of the current delegate for education who was standing behind a podium. Her mouth was open and her brow was furrowed like she was telling a life-or-death story and was at the darkest part where with one misstep the hero could be crushed. The headline was "Retiring Teachers Will Not Be Replaced." The reporter's name was Rally Kite.

"What do we care?" I asked gruffly.

"They want to put a freeze on hiring…well, what if they start firing too?"

"Wouldn't that be nice? I'd sign up to be fired."

"Dugwood would never be the same without you," said James closing the paper. "So, anyway, I can see you are determined to make a jackass of yourself with this story, but you obviously know it too. And your story is short; that's probably for the best. Whatever you do, don't give your students any juicy details that'll burn the story into their brains. You'll want to make it as forgettable as possible. What did Olga say? Something about an inner movie screen? Hang that. Keep it Zenith black and white and they'll forget you ever told them a story."

While James tried to discourage me from giving my students more ammunition to use against me, I was wondering about Rally Kite. Was he my age? Was he happily married to the woman of his dreams? Was he mortgage-free and living in a big house in Kerrisdale? Did he have a good pension? Had he published a book?

I blurted out, "She really kicked my writing dream in the gonads."

James looked at me quizzically. "Who did?"

"My mother, Adelle. That night when I took over the mortgage on my parents' house, she was wearing this dress with massive shoulder pads, out to here." I held my hands out wide past my shoulders. "She only came up to my chest. She was a tiny thing. But that day she seemed massive. She looked like an offensive lineman."

"Is she still alive?" asked James.

"She's in a care home over in West Vancouver."

"What about your dad?"

"Ken? Dead. Cancer."

"What about your ex-wife? I think you've only mentioned her once before. I don't really know anything about her."

I pressed my lips together, not really wanting to talk about the end of my marriage, but talking about my decision to go into teaching and buying my parents' house had shaken things loose. "There's not much to tell," I said flatly with a shrug.

James smirked. "I don't believe that."

"Fine." I took a deep breath. "There's this small office off the rumpus room in the basement—you've never been in there. I keep the door closed. That's where Cindy spent the last few years of our marriage, playing online games every day after we got home from school. One night, I was feeling lonely...or something...so I went downstairs and walked into her computer room without knocking. I guess she forgot to lock the door...or maybe never thought I'd come down and check on her. Anyway...she was topless and had on this pair of panties I'd never seen before. She had a small pepperoni pizza on her lap. On the computer monitor, really up close and personal, there was this bottomless fat guy, the Chicago gamer, who I will not describe for you. I went into some kind of numb rage, and, on autopilot, I waded through the garbage, picked up Cindy, the pizza box and the computer monitor, tossed them all out in the backyard, and locked her out."

"You're kidding me, right?" James was grinning, his top and bottom braces showing.

I shrugged. "I've cleared out the room, shampooed the carpets and given it a fresh coat of paint, but it still reeks like pepperoni. I'm still fighting that smell with—well never mind what with."

James banged the table with his hand laughing hard.

"Listen," he said, suddenly serious, "don't tell that part to the kids. They'll love it, but they will never forget it. And if it gets back to their parents, Caulfeild might call in the union and you could be fired—"

"Caulfeild is too busy worrying about how crisp his collar is to notice anything I'm doing."

"I'm serious, Harry," said James standing up to go. "You can't leave Dugwood. No getting fired. I need you there. Who else is going to keep me entertained?"

I looked at him, but really I was reliving the night I tossed Cindy out. I said, "They were leopard print panties. I had never seen her in anything like that before. She was always casual and earthy with me. It was the one thing about her that I found really attractive. Those panties—they're burned into my brain."

James roared and everyone at nearby tables looked over at us.

"This, you hairy beast, is why I hang out with you. You are special, seriously entertaining." He looked away from me and winked at a fresh-faced blonde who was looking up from her laptop to see what all the noise was about. "Whatever you do, don't share those details with the kids. Keep it short and colourless. Zenith black and white is the only option, if you want to come out of this with any dignity. When are you planning on performing this masochistic act anyway?"

"Monday...maybe...first thing? Or right after lunch? What do you think? I don't know...you're right. They're going to eat me alive no matter when I do it."

James zipped up his black hoody. "If it was me, which it's not, because I'm not a fuzzy, middle-aged masochist—but I get why you're bent on doing this and, listen, she's worth it—I'd do it during the last hour of the school day. They're all brain-dead in the afternoon. Chances are your story won't register at all. And if any of them do listen, it's so close to dismissal that they won't be able to focus. They might not even remember that it happened. Or they will think it was just a bad dream."

"Okay," I said, my guts suddenly off and bubbling. "I'll do it when they are mostly zoned out, and then when I bomb—do you think she'll care if I bomb? She'll just be impressed that I'm trying. Right?"

"Who? Olga? Yeah. Go for it, Beast!" James smiled tightly, not showing his braces, then steered the conversation back to my story. "Don't take this too seriously. You're not going to teach them anything about mortgages or career choices or happiness. Don't destroy what little respect those kids might still have for you. Think about it. It's only mid-February. There are four months left, and you can't count on a strike to save you."

"If I flop, do I still give myself credit for the learning outcomes?"

"Hang the lesson plan. Just get it over with. Five minutes, no panties, no pepperoni, just black and white." James was about to leave.

"Can I ask you something?" I said, cautiously.

James nodded. "If you're quick. I'm meeting my dad for lunch."

"What did you mean when you said I should go for it?"

James shrugged. "I mean she's nice, but—"

"You're not going to ask her out again," I stated, trying to make him commit to it.

"Relax, Beast. She's just a woman—a very attractive one—but still just a woman. And if you can get her, she's all yours. I'm going to stick to dating kindergarten teachers and hot waitresses and lonely, pretty writers at coffee shops." He hesitated dramatically before adding with a gentlemanly bow: "I'm out."

When James was gone, I ordered another coffee and cracked open a well-worn copy of *The Catcher in the Rye*. Though it was a go-to read for me, I could not get Olga off my mind. The novel just seemed too bitter to match my new found optimism. James was out. I had a chance.

That afternoon, I marked twenty-seven really weak short stories. Then, lifted as I was by this new floaty, optimistic feeling about James being out and Olga being a possibility, I found myself having my semi-annual urge to reach out to my mother, Adelle. She and I had been inmates of my father, Ken, who was a handsome pilot twenty years her senior. While he dashed around the world in his irresistible uniform, Adelle and I co-existed, first in an apartment in West Vancouver, then later in our big house in Kerrisdale which my parents built in the late sixties. We moved in when I was six. Then, fourteen years later, the house was mine. These cyclical urges to call my mother were not something that I could put into words. They were deep, inexplicable desires that came from the ancient part of my brain or those raw places on my heart that still ached on rainy days. Nine times out of ten I could suppress them. I would stop myself by remembering who

Adelle really was, not who I hoped she had been. Since preschool I had known how little she wanted me. Her neglect of everything except my most basic needs was obvious, and when Ken was flying, she didn't try to hide it. But my fail-safe memories didn't always work. So, on some kind of emotional autopilot, I called Canterbury Care Home and foolishly reached out to her.

When Adelle came on the line, I launched into my story, just as I had told it to James that morning at Jitters. There was a long stretch of silence when I finished.

"Hello?" I said, wondering if she was still there.

Her voice was faint. "I loved that royal blue wool dress with the shoulder pads so much," she said. "And, after than night, I never wore it again. It was all your fault, Harold. You ruined that dress."

I ignored the attack and asked her if there was anything else she could remember about that night. She answered by asking me if I still lived in *her* house and if I still drove that embarrassing orange car. I told her I was guilty on both accounts and hung up.

3

At two in the afternoon on Monday, when my students were supposed to be brain-dead, I got up from the safety of my desk and went to the front of the classroom. It was warm for February and the heat was still cranked up. I could feel sweat soaking into the fabric of my shirt. The low afternoon sun stabbed into the room, backlighting the students. It looked like they all had bright, positive auras and halos, but they didn't. No one noticed that I had gotten up from my desk and was standing by the projector at the front of the room. They kept talking, not bothering to whisper or give any sign that they respected my authority.

"Ahem," I said, ending the math lesson by switching off the projector. "Eyes front, please."

The volume rose slightly.

"Tyler and Dylan, turn around, please, and listen."

The boys glanced over their shoulders at me and went back to talking.

"Class," I said as I ran my sweaty palms against my vest, "I'm going to tell you a story about a kind of death."

"Beast," snorted Alexa, the long-haired alpha girl. "Its pits are gross."

"Gross," said Lauren, Alexa's second-in-command. "I'm going to barf."

"Students, eyes front, mouths closed." I was determined. The students just didn't know it yet.

The winter sun slouched behind a cloud, and the room darkened and cooled, but not enough to suck the sweat back into my armpits. I took a deep breath and remembered the workshop, the candle, the darkened room, Olga's smile and her bare feet. I went over to the open classroom door. I closed it assertively, with a firm slam. The students stopped talking. They were all staring at me. Under their questioning gazes, I turned off the lights and took off my shoes.

I announced, "I'm going to tell you a true story about death, the death of a dream."

"Whatever…," murmured Alexa.

The class giggled at me, but I didn't back down. I stood and delivered my story pretty much in the same way I had told it to James at the coffee shop and to Adelle on the phone and to myself in the shower that morning. I fired up the memory in my imagination; then I put my head down and let the words spew out over the kids. Heeding James's advice I didn't mention the pizza or panties, but I did add the detail about my mother's royal blue dress with the shoulder pads. Some of the kids actually laughed out loud at that part. And, I noticed, they weren't laughing at me, they were simply laughing; it was a disarmed, genuine laugh reflecting a shared moment of pleasure. I felt it, and it surprised me. At that moment I sort of liked them.

Five minutes later, when it was over, the students were still. None of them spoke, not even the cheekiest ones. They just stared at me, backlit again by the sun which had come out during my story.

I broke the silence with, "Like I said a few minutes ago, this is a story about the death of a dream, my dream of being a writer, an editor and a novelist, in exchange for a fancy house I never really wanted. In fact, that's the title we'll give it: 'Death of a Dream.'"

Silence still.

"Does anyone have any questions," I asked, still in my sock feet with the lights off, wondering what horrors were to come once they found their voices and relit their sense of haughty entitlement, "about mortgages or careers or making tough decisions?"

Otto Logan's hand shot up. This was encouraging. Otto was normally not present at all.

"You need a new shirt, Mr. Tyke," he said earnestly. "You must be very uncomfortable."

The whole class burst out laughing.

I turned on the lights, opened the door and picked up my shoes. I carried them back to the safety of my desk. I said, "The bell goes in twenty minutes. Get started on your short story revisions. No talking, please. I want them handed in first thing tomorrow."

"But I thought they were due next week," whined Alexa, her head tilted so that her long brown hair fell to one side.

"They were," I said with a deliberate edge. "Now they're due tomorrow." I didn't like my class any more. The shared moment of pleasant laughter was dead.

"Not fair," said Alexa.

"No, it's not," I snapped. "Life isn't, not once you get out on your own. You should get used to it." Then, just because I could,

I added, "And, class, you are going to have to read your rewritten stories out loud in front of everyone tomorrow."

The room exploded with protest. I felt good about that. Let them sweat.

After the bell rang, James popped in. He was dying to know how it had gone. I expressed frustration with not being able to reach the students, and he gave me an I-told-you-so speech and encouraged me to leave it alone and not do any more damage. Storytelling, he said, was for primary school teachers and librarians not for grade-six teachers. He told me I should be more like him and stock up on digital learning materials and embrace the school's One Laptop Per Child campaign. He said I should forget about sharing tales from the personal life of a miserable, middle-aged teacher who, ironically, and despite a nasty divorce, lives in a very nice house in one of the nicest parts of town. He reminded me that my interest in storytelling was about dating a storyteller, nothing more. He said I should be honest with myself, that I should man up and ask the woman out before I had a meltdown. He was right. I had to man up and ask her out. I had to, or my last bit of hope for happiness would shrivel up and fall off.

That evening, I sat down at my computer in the main-floor office that used to be my father's. I was fiddling with a piece of paper, the handout from Olga's workshop; on one side was a headshot of Olga. I stared at her face, studying the line of her cheek bones and the curve of her lips for a long time, before flipping the page over and re-reading her storytelling tips. I wanted to email her and tell her that I had used her advice to tell my class a story. But how could I say it without coming off as just another guy fishing for a date with a pretty woman?

I spent an hour searching online for a photo, a website, anything about her. The only thing I found was a newspaper article written in Spanish. There was a picture of Olga with a dozen Mexican children in a room constructed of unpainted cinderblock walls, a dirt floor and a grass roof. The headline was: *Increíble mujer enseña matemáticas sólo narrando cuentos,* or "Extraordinary Woman Teaches Math Just With Stories." I couldn't agree more. With her hair pulled back in a low pony tail, her bone structure was model perfect. She was extraordinary— beautiful beyond imagining. I enlarged the image to fit my entire computer screen and stared at what I knew was the most beautiful face a woman could ever have. She was smiling gracefully with just the right amount of teeth showing. I was dying to kiss that smile.

It took me four hours to come up with this:

Dear Olga, I tried telling a story to my students today. It didn't go very well. Do you think you could help me? Harry Tyke.

I stared at those three sentences for a long time, until I unbuttoned my vest and took it off. Feeling freer and bolder, I took off my sweat-stained shirt too. With a surge of confidence I wrote my story down for her. Was I a writer? I didn't know if I still was, but I did my best to tell her a good story. I hadn't meant to write it all down, but once I got started, I just wrote. When I was done, I read it through and realized that I had added a huge amount of detail—vivid detail, good sensory stuff like Olga had talked about in her workshop. The more I relived the memory of the evening that had set the course of my life, the more I remembered. It had all come back as I was writing: the dry, eggy taste of the overcooked Yorkshire pudding, the silky sensation of the green shag carpet on my sock feet, the velvet sofas, that it was raining that night, that it was chilly in the house, that the house smelled like charcoal, that my mother's voice was raspy from smoking. And I just poured the words into the email.

As I was fussing over the last comma in the last sentence the phone rang. It was James, but I didn't feel like talking to anyone so I let the machine get it. The ringing and James's voice— coupled with thoughts about his date with Olga—broke the spell of my confidence.

I saved the email in my drafts folder and shut down the computer.

4

Early the next morning, still damp from the shower, I stood in my walk-in closet, the same closet where Adelle had once hung her royal blue dress with the shoulder pads and Cindy had once heaped her clothes in motley piles of clean and dirty. I examined the row of faded dress shirts and tired sweater vests that hung on wire hangers. Cindy believed wire hangers were cheap and would only use expensive wooden ones, even though she rarely hung anything up. After she left, I bagged up all the wooden hangers and drove them to the local hospice thrift store. That was about as radical as I ever was when it came to acting on my feelings—except for the day I put her out on the back stoop in her leopard-print panties. Otherwise, I was quite contained emotionally, though I wasn't that particular morning. The strange sweetish sensation was back, the same one I experienced the morning of Olga's workshop. I was thick in the throat and bubbling in the intestines.

Still naked, I went back to the bathroom. I trimmed the straggling hairs in my beard. Then, as I leaned towards the mirror for closer inspection, I noticed something for the first time: my stomach was wet on the underside. I looked down. A great, flabby roll rested on the countertop like a dead animal. I lifted the thing up and patted it dry with a fraying, over-washed hand towel, wiped the water and whiskers off the countertop, and went back to the walk-in to find something that suited my mood. When I did find something, I spent a long time in front of the full-length closet mirror tucking my shirt into my jeans with unusual vigour, trying to make the fabric function as a girdle. Still unsatisfied with my choice in attire, I went back to the bathroom and looked at my face. I suddenly felt like the beard had to go, but I wasn't that brave. Instead, I shaved it so that it took up less real estate on my cheeks and neck.

Before I left for school, I turned on the computer, which took longer than usual to boot up. The waiting was uncomfortable. When the computer eventually finished torturing me, I opened my drafts folder and re-read the email I had written to Olga. It seemed okay. Actually, the story was quite good, well told, I thought. I sat for a while drinking coffee, wondering if I should send the email as it was, or if I should rewrite it, just because. In the end, I only changed "I tried telling a story to my students *today*" to "I tried telling a story to my students *yesterday*." And I sent it.

I arrived at school half an hour early, which was rare for me back then. Over the decades, I had cut my arrival time down with the same degree of precision that Lamborghini cuts its leather for the interior of its supercars. I could park at eight forty-three and be at my desk at precisely eight forty-five when the second bell rang. It was strange to be at my desk so early, leafing through my agenda and getting worksheets and handouts in order. I usually did that while the students were filing in. First up was PE, then Math. After recess, I would start hearing their revised short stories, read aloud. I would fit in as many of those as I could before lunch. The afternoon would be silent reading and computer lab, where I had to review online safety for a district-wide test that was coming up. It had to do with a new bill being proposed by the Education Agency, but as yet, we (I mean "we the teachers") didn't have all the details.

I leaned back in my chair. It groaned like an animal, which reminded me of the pinkish roll of hairy blubber I had seen lying on my bathroom counter. I got up and went down to the staff-room for a coffee refill. Marigold Lovitt, the school counsellor, was doing the same. She was adding sugar to a tall travel mug that said: *Those who tell the stories rule society.*

"Where did you get that?" I asked.

"Good morning, Harry," she said, screwing the lid on the mug and picking it up. "This?" She pointed at the quote. "My daughter brought it back from university for me. It was in my Christmas stocking. She's so thoughtful."

"How is she liking the creative writing program?" I asked.

"She adores it. It's inspirational, she says. She's already finished her first novel and gave me a copy of the first draft to read. It's based on my grandmother's life, her struggles as a young girl growing up in Saskatoon during the Depression." The counsellor looked dreamily at the mug.

I flinched with jealousy as I put the cream back in the refrigerator. I hated that Marigold Lovitt's daughter was living my dream. But, instead of retreating into my usual silent sulkiness, I asked dryly, "What's it called?"

Marigold smiled and said with twinkle-eyed pride, *"Dry Love."*

I nodded, faked a smile and started walking out of the staffroom.

Marigold grabbed my arm and stopped me. With that prideful twinkle, she said, "I saw Otto Logan after school on Friday. He told me you took your shoes off in class and turned off the lights, and you told the class a story about your mother playing football."

I couldn't help smiling, genuinely, this time. "Something like that. I told them about the day life my went down the toilet."

Marigold raised an eyebrow and lowered her chin with disapproval at my mention of the word toilet. Her disapproval annoyed me. Weren't teachers allowed to talk openly about toilets?

"My mother," I continued, "happened to be wearing a blue dress with shoulders pads that made her look like an offensive lineman. It was the eighties. I doubt you remember. How old were you then? Ten?"

"You'd be surprised what I remember about those days, Harry," she laughed. Otto went on and on about those shoulder pads for our whole session. He's asked me, 'since I'm old,' to wear a dress like that to school so he can see what it looks like. He is obsessed with knowing how they sew shoulder pads into clothing."

"Of course he is." I was well aware of Otto's obsessive tendencies about clothing and video games. Since September it had been the colour orange and Mindblocks. Now it was shoulder pads in women's clothing.

The morning passed uneventfully—PE, Math, poorly rewritten short stories recited by nervous students, through which I daydreamed about Olga. When would she write back? What would she think of my story? As soon as the kids were eating lunch, I checked my email and immediately wished I hadn't. Seeing no reply from Olga was devastating, so I stormed outside to the parking lot and got in my car and pouted. Then James came out, tapped on the passenger side window and made things worse.

"You look grim today, Beast. Mind if I join you?"

I waved him into the passenger seat.

James asked as he sat down next to me and slammed the door shut, "Did you get Olga's email?"

"How do you know I emailed her?"

James looked at me blankly. "You did?"

Realizing he was talking about something else, I asked, quickly, to cover up, "What email?"

"The follow-up email…," he said, looking at me like I was clueless.

I shrugged.

"From the workshop…"

I shrugged again.

"Don't sweat it, Beast. I'm sure it wasn't on purpose. Maybe you gave her the wrong email address. I'll forward it to you later."

I forced myself to ask, "When did you get it?"

"Last night," he said.

The afternoon was misery for me. I felt rejected down to my core. I tried to tell myself that maybe I had written down the wrong email address at the workshop. Had I? It didn't seem likely, so I couldn't help but feel slighted, rejected, second class. I was in no mood for games when chaos broke out in the computer lab two seconds before I was about to start the review for the online safety test. The power went out, shutting all the computers down and blackening the windowless room. Eleven and twelve-year-olds think they can get away with murder in the dark, and my class started in immediately.

"Ugly, hairy beast!" went the rhythmical chant, accompanied by desk drumming.

"Settle down, please," I said, keeping a heavy lid on my Olga-related frustrations. "The lights will be back on in a moment." Dugwood emergency protocol stated that in the event of a power failure classes were to stay where they were until an administrator came by to give instructions, which meant I was stuck in the computer lab, in the near-dark, with the yard apes and mean girls until the principal or vice principal came by.

"Don't touch me, pervert!" said one of the girls, laughing.

It was Alexa. "Keep your hands to yourself, please," I said. "And, Alexa, be quiet."

"Sorry, Beast," she said loudly.

The room popped with laughter and echoes of "sorry, Beast," which soon morphed into more chanting and drumming:

"Ugly, hairy beast. Ugly, hairy beast. Ugly, hairy—"

I slammed the palm of my right hand down on the table in front of me. The noise level dropped enough for me to bark, "Enough! Be quiet, or you will all be staying after school today to work on your short stories."

Tyler piped up right away. "You can't do that! I've got game club after school. My ride will leave without me."

"So be it," I said. "If you don't settle down, you are all staying late today and rewriting your stories, properly." The darkness ballooned with groans.

"Why don't you tell us your story?" said a hyper voice from the back of the room. It was Otto Logan.

The room went quiet.

"What story?" I said, playing dumb.

"The story you told us yesterday," said Otto.

"Yeah!" shouted a few of the others.

I lied, "I didn't tell you a story yesterday."

Alexa spoke up. "Yes, you did! The one about how your parents made you be a teacher."

The beast in me wanted revenge. "Did I tell you about that? How strange. I don't recall that at all. Why would I share such a personal story with you? You don't respect me. I know you don't care about me. I'm not even a person to you—I'm a beast: a big, ugly, hairy, beast!"

"The story about the blue dress with shoulder pads!" yelled Otto. He was getting really worked up. He was squatting on his chair and bouncing with terrible energy. "Don't lie, Mr. Tyke! You told us the story yesterday!"

"I did no such thing. You're experiencing a mass delusion."

"C'mon, Mr. Tyke," said Alexa. "Please tell us the story again."

"Please, Mr. Tyke," echoed her classmates.

I grinned, knowing my face was mostly hidden in the dark. I had them. "Do you remember the title of my story?"

"Being a Teacher Sucks?" said Tyler.

"The Shoulder Pads?" said Otto.

"Death of a Dream," stated Alexa, the cheeky tone completely absent.

In the dark of the computer lab, in the fresh quiet of the room, I slipped off my shoes and told my story a second time. This time I really got into it. Freed by the darkness, and in an unconscious attempt to emulate the beautiful storyteller who had apparently slighted me, rejected me and made me feel second-class, I let the story fly and I mean fly—

I was interrupted partway through by someone knocking on the door. I stopped mid-sentence. It was the principal, Nash Caulfeild. The lights would be out for the rest of the day, which was only another twenty minutes. I was to take the students back to our classroom and dismiss them at the regular time.

Back in the classroom, the students were not willing to let me off the hook. They were keen to hear the rest of the story. So in the grey light, in my sock feet, I went on and on and on. The more I told of that life-altering Sunday evening in 1981, the more I remembered every sight, sound, smell, taste, and touch, and I heaped on vivid detail, without restraint, so that my young listeners could visualize my parents, the furniture, the room temperature, the sound of the cuckoo clock ticking on the fireplace mantle, the smells of smoke and charred beef, the feel of the knots in my stomach. By the end of the tale, which ended several minutes after the bell rang for dismissal, that particular snapshot of my life was etched, burned, carved into the meat of their video game-addled brains. I had told the tale with full-colour, movie-screen vividness so that the students would be able to retell it.

And they did.

5

"What exactly, Mr. Tyke, did you believe you would accomplish by recounting for your students a story that includes walking in on your ex-wife in her—was it zebra-striped undergarments?" asked Nash Caulfeild, our no-nonsense, Ivy-League principal. The man, a Brit and former Olympic rugby player, who was younger than me and an inch taller, rested his elbows on his desk and was, one at a time, unclipping his cufflinks and meticulously rolling up his sleeves, making sure that each fold was three fingers wide.

"They were leopard print, actually," I said plainly, after clearing my throat.

Keeping his eyes locked on his immaculate white cuffs, Caulfeild said, "Now, it seems, every child in the school, from Janet's kindergarten class to Bill's seventh-grade rugby team, is aware of that particular detail from your rather sorry life, as are all the parents who rang me this morning to complain about you." He turned a notepad around so that I could read the long list of last names. "In the last hour, I have been contacted personally by each of these families. Mrs. Peach, Alexa's mother, has threatened to go to the local papers. You do realize this is a royal cock up, Mr. Tyke. They want your head. They want you gone. And, quite frankly, after this display of adolescent behaviour, so do I. We have a reputation for respect at Dugwood."

I almost laughed out loud and rolled my eyes, but, out of respect, I did neither.

He went on in his high-and-mighty tone, "And I'm not going to let you tarnish it, not one inch of it. I have phone calls in to both the union and the superintendent's office to find out what exactly I can do to you."

I leaned back in the chair, stroked my beard, and looked out the window behind Caulfeild's head at the mountains. Caulfeild leaned back, too. He cocked his head a little to one side and chuckled at me. I couldn't stand the man, and as for Dugwood having a reputation for respect, Caulfield was delusional. This generation of kids, and many of my colleagues, sadly, didn't know what the basic definition of respect was, nor did they seem to care. It was an antiquated notion, old-school, and, apparently, not worth teaching or learning these days.

"What is it you cannot eat anymore, Mr. Tyke?" Caulfield asked.

"Pizza, pepperoni pizza."

"And why is that?"

I jerked to my feet, put my hands on the principal's desk, and leaned over so that our faces were really close, just a few inches apart. My roll of blubber—which was straining at the fabric of the one-size-too-small shirt I had put on that morning—threatened to flop onto his desk like a fat fist. This amped up my anger to another level altogether.

"Because the room that she gamed out in was full of half-empty pizza boxes and everything was rotten. It was stinking and rotten. Just like my students' teeth are rotten, and their minds are rotten with laziness and disrespect and games, games, games, and more games. I've had it. I wish the whole school—no!—the whole system—would...ha ha...reboot—so that we could start fresh! We need to send the self-centred little tyrants back to their gamed-out parents, with their online affairs, and they can all game out together until their eyes bleed, and they stink up the whole city with rotten food and poor hygiene and bad manners!" I pushed off my fingertips, which were bright red and puffy, and pointed down at Caulfeild, who was sitting there with an odd look on his face, like he was going to burst out laughing. "You can do whatever you want with me. The whole thing is just—" I stopped.

Caulfeild was smiling openly now, his ribs shaking with barely suppressed amusement.

I walked out of the school into the cold, February day. The sky was clear. I could see the North Shore mountains, stark white and deep green, set in jagged relief against the rare, sharp-blue sky. I wanted to pick up the tallest one and hurl it into the sea. I went to my car, but I couldn't find my keys. They were in the pocket of my trench coat which was up in my classroom, and so, giving in entirely to my frustrations, I pounded the hood of my orange, 1986 Plymouth Horizon until it had a dent in it the shape of my fist.

James came out of the school carrying my coat. "Here," he said tossing it on my heaving back. "Caulfeild says you should go home and pull yourself together. Take a sick day." He paused. "Maybe you should go buy yourself a new car…or just get some bodywork done…listen, just get out of here and let it blow over. You know the kids. They don't remember much of anything. Same goes for their parents. It'll blow over."

The trench coat slid off my back. James picked it up and handed it to me. "Take it, Harry. Go home. Read a novel."

I snapped the coat out of his hand. The rage and anxiety I was feeling was still fresh in my body. I wasn't going to be so easily talked in off the ledge.

I said to James, "I went big screen. It's like they were there with me, that Labour Day Sunday in my parents' living room and that Saturday night when I tossed Cindy out the basement door. They were there. They lived it with me. They are never going to forget it, nor are their parents."

James looked at me, shrugged and smiled. "You're making me wish I'd been there to hear it. It sounds like you told a great story."

"Yeah, right," I said as I unlocked the car door. It groaned as it swung open. I ducked in, sat down in the driver's seat, slammed the door shut and started the car. I rolled down the window and yelled, "You didn't forward that email from Olga to me yet."

"Okay. Okay. I'll do that now." He shook his head and grinned. "Maybe you should try using your newfound storytelling powers for good instead of evil," yelled James as I backed wildly out of the parking stall, almost clipping him. "And, hey, you've got a great story to tell her. She'll love it!"

I screeched out of the parking lot. I didn't stop and buy a new car or take my hatchback in for bodywork. I drove to Jitters.

The sharp, aromatic smell of fresh-ground coffee brought me back to reality.

"Hi, Mr. Tyke," said an unfamiliar staff member with a fresh face.

I smiled and nodded as I picked up a copy of the newspaper and got in line to order. There were three people ahead of me and the place was almost full like it was on Saturday morning. I was surprised and irritated.

As I flipped through the paper and shuffled along in the line, I thought about Olga.

"Hi, Mr. Tyke," said the fresh face when I got up to the counter. "You're not at school today. You didn't retire yet, did you?"

I knew she was a former student, but I couldn't pull her name. "No. Not yet," I said. "Just taking the day off."

"Guess what?" she said as she gave me my change. "Today is my first day, and my last day, working here."

"How so?"

"Well, I got this job at the exact same time as I was applying to do animation for a gaming company, and I just got that job too, so I'm quitting here and starting there on Monday."

"Congratulations," I said with a fake smile. "The world certainly needs more video game designers."

"Yeah. It does. It totally does. Everything out there sucks. Nice to see you, Mr. Tyke. Have a great day."

As I went around the counter and picked up my coffee, I saw *her* in line: Olga, the hot storyteller. She was in my Jitters on a mid-week morning, looking hot in her skinny jeans with tall black leather boots and a black turtle neck partially covered by a purple sweater that draped off her slim shoulders like a toga. Sweat leaked out of me, my throat got sticky and tight, my guts churned double-time, and the coffee cup trembled in my thick, ungraceful hand.

Less than a minute later, I was in my car, driving home, with coffee sloshing on the crumb-filled floor mats from the lidless cup. Olga was out of my league. That was my story, and I was sticking to it.

When I got home, I took the remains of my coffee to the bathroom and ran water for a bath. As the tub filled, I went to my office and checked my voice mail. There was a message from Principal Caulfeild: I was to return to the school immediately. They couldn't find a sub for my class, and the vice principal and the principal both had commitments and could not cover for me. Too bad for them. I wasn't going back, and I wasn't going to call and tell them. Then, deciding to skip the bath for the moment, I went to the bathroom, shut the water off, went to my office, and sat down with my cold coffee. I looked out the office window at the backyard. The lawn and garden needed tending. The coach house needed a fresh coat of paint. And it had clouded over. When I finally had the courage to check my inbox, there were three emails from Olga. I felt like I could finally breathe. One was the follow-up email that James had just forwarded to me, one was the same follow-up email sent by Olga herself, the other email was in reply to my email.

I opened it first. It read:

Hi Harry. Thank you for sharing your story with me. You are a good writer, and I think you have a lot of great, juicy imagery in your story. I can see why you wanted be a novelist. You'd be great at it. I am sorry to hear that it didn't go well with your students. It could be because you were not relaxed and in the moment. Did you do any voices or facial expressions? Remember that exercise we did where we went around the circle exaggerating the sounds of our names? Remember how much we all enjoyed watching each other take a risk like that? It's really entertaining to see someone get into a story with such passion and intensity that they actually become the character. If I were you, I'd try telling it again and adding some character voices. You did a great job with that in our workshop exercises, and your students will be completely engaged. They'll love it. I promise. Let me know how you do. By the way, good for you for sharing a story from your life. I am certain that like most people our age, you have a great deal of wisdom to share. Go for it, and, please, keep me in your story circle. Sincerely, Olga.

"People our age," I said aloud. Our age? She looked much younger than me, but I liked the way she said it; it was flirtatious. I leaned back and imagined what it would be like to hold Olga's hand, to kiss her. I closed my eyes and took a few good, deep breaths. I stopped mid-inhale—the chair didn't just smell like old leather and cigarettes; it smelled like stale pepperoni pizza. At first, I thought it was just my imagination, but then I put my nose right into the leather and inhaled again. It smelled like Cindy's computer room in the basement. She had used this chair for her all-night gaming sessions, demoting my rear end to a kitchen chair. It had been something of a victory for me—like reaping the spoils of war—that night when I locked her out and carried the leather office chair back upstairs where it belonged.

Elated by Olga's reply, but annoyed by the pepperoni smell in my leather chair, I went and took my bath, with a printed copy of Olga's email in hand. I read it over again, and with each kind word, each flirtatious tone, I felt my bulk relax, my emotions reign back in.

The phone rang three times in the next fifteen minutes. When I finally got out of the tub and answered it, the school secretary said they needed me back immediately. The education assistant they had put in charge of my class was in tears. I wasn't surprised.

When I pulled into the teachers' parking lot at Dugwood, recess had just ended and Principal Caulfeild was standing outside the front doors waiting for me. As soon as I got out of my car, he was on me.

"I need to discuss terms with you before you go up to your classroom, Mr. Tyke," he said to me as I got out of the car.

"What terms?"

I could see he was trying to use his one-inch advantage to make it look like he was towering over me. I stepped up to him.

He held his ground and said, "If I hear that you have been teaching with anything other than an approved curriculum resource, you will be disciplined. Do you understand, Mr. Tyke? No more stories." The gauntlet had been thrown.

I picked it up. "No problem," I lied as I brushed past him and went inside humming the Do-Re-Mi scale up and down to warm up my vocal cords. On the drive back to school, I had remembered back to Olga's workshop, back to the part where we had done the voice exercises. It was one of Olga's secrets to telling a memorable story—use your voice. And we had. After our opera singer warm up, she had us back in our circle around the candle. I hadn't been nervous at first about the exercise—playing with the vowel and consonant sounds in your first and last name as you say it out loud for the group—but when Olga did her demonstration, my guts twisted up in the most uncomfortable way. When it was my turn, I had been quite conservative with my sounds. It was embarrassing to let go like that in front of other teachers. But, I thought, as I walked into my classroom, looking like a fool didn't really apply to me anymore.

Otto Logan exploded out of his seat when I walked in. Affecting a high-pitched lady's voice, I said, "Sit down, Otto!"

The classroom fell silent, instantly. The young lady who had been babysitting my class smiled weakly and walked out. Otto sat down. The students were looking at me but not saying anything.

I shut the door, turned out the lights, took my shoes off and said in a deep, powerful voice, "Pens down. Polly, please stop writing on your hand. Listen to my story, class. Listen and see it. Listen and feel it. Listen and remember so that this does not happen to you." I lowered my tone and quieted my voice and began:

"It was a miserable Sunday evening on Labour Day weekend in 1981. It was pouring rain outside." I went over to a front-row desk and beat it softly with the pads of my fingertips to imitate the sound of rainfall. I drummed softly as I spoke. "I was twenty and loving my job as a junior copy editor and the fact that I was not in school anymore. I was making seven-fifty an hour, which was okay back then because I was still living at home with my parents—my dad Ken, a pilot, and my mother Adelle, an aging debutante who chain-smoked and made a horrible roast beef dinner every Sunday night. We lived in large house in Kerrisdale, on a manicured street lined with stately elm trees. The house was prime real estate—four bedrooms, three bathrooms, three floors, a coach house and big lot."

I stopped drumming suddenly and turned up the volume.

"The whole house smelled like burnt roast beef and stale cigarettes. We were sitting at the dining room table. It was glass and round and had three settings of magenta placemats, and white china with a genuine silver rim around the edges of the plates. We each had two crystal glasses: one for water, one for wine. Both of mine were empty. My plate was swimming with lumpy dark-brown gravy and charred slivers of beef. I was full and queasy and wanted to go upstairs and watch a video. I was carrying my plate across the shag carpet to the kitchen, when my father said"—I dropped my tone and adopted a wheeze, saying in my father's raspy voice: "Harry, come and sit down with us in the living room."

"So I went into the kitchen, handed my plate to my mother, who, in her royal blue dress with shoulder pads out to here, was silently rinsing dishes before putting them in the dishwasher, and then followed my father to the living room."

Otto jerked to his feet at the mention of the dress with shoulder pads. I motioned for him to sit down. And the boy did.

"My mother followed me into the living room. I sat on one sofa. My parents sat at opposite ends of the matching one on the other side of the coffee table. I remember thinking that was strange because they usually sat right beside each other. My mother was clearly distant, upset..."

Here I dove completely into character. I pulled up a stool, sat down, and for the next few minutes I was Ken again, saying: "Well, Harold. You are twenty years old now, and it's time you got serious about your future. Your mother and I feel that this writing dream of yours is never going to amount to anything. We are moving to New Mexico, and we want you to have the house. Now, here's the deal, Sonny Boy, there's one condition. You have to have a job with a pension, a good one, and there's nothing better than a government pension. So we've decided you should go into teaching."

I had them, my students. Every pair of eyes was on me.

Suddenly inspired, I said, "Put your desks in a circle. Quickly, please."

They quickly obeyed. The classroom was loud with scraping noises as the students dragged their desks across the floor. I walked into the middle and continued.

"Even at just twenty years old, I was smart enough to know I could never afford a big house like that on my own. It was already worth half a million dollars. My parents were offering me the deal of a lifetime. They were going to let me buy it by paying rent to them one month at a time. It was a one-in-a-million deal, and I knew I should take it, but I didn't want to become a teacher. I hated school. I hated kids. I wanted to write. So, I made my case—in the living room with the green shag and the burned roast beef smell—I told them that editing for a newspaper was a good fit for me, that I didn't even like kids, that I hated school—"

At that point, I was completely inside the memory of that night and I yelled, "It's my life! I don't need this stinking house!"

I stopped. I was breathing hard. Tears bulged out from the corners of my eyes. It was dead quiet for a moment.

"What about your ex-wife, Mr. Tyke?" asked Alexa. "Can you tell us that part again?"

"No," I said, walking back to my desk.

Lauren put her hand up.

"You've got to finish the story, Mr. Tyke," she said.

"Not today," I said. "Put your desks back where they belong."

The classroom was loud again with scraping noises as the students dragged their desks across the floor and put them back in rows.

"I still don't get it," said Tyler as he plunked himself back down.

"What don't you get?" I asked.

"You said you don't like kids," said Tyler.

"I don't," I said, making direct eye contact with the boy.

"Why not?" asked Otto Logan.

"You're in trouble, Mr. Tyke," said Alexa. "You can't say stuff like that."

"Yes, he can," said Tyler. "It's just a story."

"No, it's his real life," said Lauren.

"Is it?" said Tyler.

Dylan put his hand straight up in the air. I had never seen him so enthusiastic before. "Mr. Tyke! Mr. Tyke!"

"Yes, Dylan."

"Is your house an asset or a liability?"

I admit, the question caught me off guard, but I was fairly sure of the answer. "It's an asset because I own it, and it's going up in value—"

Dylan eagerly interrupted me. "My dad says that the house you live in is never an asset because it doesn't make you money unless you like rent it out or something…"

I flicked on the lights, opened the door to let some air in, and put my shoes back on. I might not be happy with the decision I had been pressured into making all those years ago, but my house was an asset. Other than my car, it was all I owned; all my savings were tied up in it.

"Right, thank you, Dylan. Now, please open your math books," I said. "We're going to talk about percentages today, and I'm going to show you how to calculate a downpayment and a mortgage." I paused. No. No books. "Everyone, stop," I said, holding my hand up. "Put your books away, clear your desks."

"But I want to take notes," whined Alexa.

"No notes, just use your brain. Trust yourself that you are smart enough to remember this stuff."

"I'm not," said Otto.

Everyone laughed.

"Yes, you are, Otto," I said. "Use the story."

While the students reluctantly, and noisily, put away their binders, I thought back to Olga's storytelling workshop and how that nearly empty, darkened drama room, the circle of chairs around the candle, the shoes-off rule had made me feel. I searched for just the right words to express it. In two words it was—creative and adventurous—or was it free?

The class was getting very noisy. So, in the spirit of being creatively adventurous and free, I said, "Okay, class, we are going to talk about mort-ga-ges," and when I said the word, I chopped it up into chunks of sound so that it was stretched out over forty-five seconds. I exaggerated each part of it, speaking softly for one syllable, turning up the volume for the next. I had their attention, and by the end of the lesson, I knew that every one of those kids could tell you what a mortgage was, even the alpha mean girl, even the lead yard ape, even Mr. Mindblocks. They had it.

6

As I was packing up to go home for the day, an unexpected visitor appeared in the doorway of my classroom. It was Mrs. Peach, Alexa's mother. She was smiling, but I didn't believe for one moment that she wasn't concealing pepper spray under the lapel of her white leather coat.

"I don't have time for a meeting right now," I said, putting my trench coat on.

"I just need a moment of your time, Mr. Tyke," said Mrs. Peach. She seemed to be trying to block the doorway with her anorexic frame.

I almost laughed out loud.

She said, her expression tense, "Alexa just informed myself and some of the other parents that you told the students your—," she pursed her lips for a second, then forced out the word, "—story."

I turned off my classroom lights and said, politely, "Please get out of my way, Mrs. Peach."

Mrs. Peach pushed her flat chest out at me and rolled back her bony shoulders, clearly trying to take up enough space to hinder my exit. "My husband and I have talked to a lawyer—"

"I know you have talked to a lawyer," I said, abruptly. "Principal Caulfield told me this morning, but the thing is, Mrs. Peach, you don't realize who you are dealing with."

She smiled, harshly and confidently, and pronounced haughtily, "In fact, Mr. Tyke, we know perfectly well who we are dealing with. You are an unhealthy, angry, middle-aged man who is experiencing a cognitive break from reality. You are a vulgar, shallow man who has lost his sense of right and wrong, appropriate and inappropriate." Though she kept her composure as she spoke, her mouth and eyes began to widen, looking grotesquely animated in her gaunt, pale face.

"If Alexa told you my entire story last night, then you must know that the smell of rancid pepperoni still haunts the room where my ex-wife used to do her thing with her online lover. And, if you actually listened to the story your daughter told you, you would know that I have tried with tremendous effort to get that smell out of my life."

She was about to speak, but I held up my hand to silence her and continued. "But, here is something my students don't know, a little nugget I did not share with them. I didn't put this in my story—and maybe I should have, to teach them about perseverance, about determination. You see…how should I put this so that you will understand?"

She raised a painted-on eyebrow at me.

"I use that room, Mrs. Peach, to pass gas."

She took a half-step back. "What do you mean pass gas?"

"I mean pass gas—flatulence."

Mrs. Peach grimaced and lifted her gloved hand in front of her mouth and sharp nose as if she could smell me right at that very moment.

I had her on the ropes and was loving it. "Twice a day I go into that empty room, close the door, and pass gas. I've been relentless, driven. But the room still smells like pepperoni. And you know what? I'll never give up. I'll go home right now with my churning guts and light a stink bomb in there, because someday, Mrs. Peach, I will defeat that smell and all the other bad smells in my world."

Mrs. Peach still had her gloved hand up in front of her nose and mouth. I could see bits of her overly-lipsticked mouth through the spaces between her skinny fingers.

In a muffled, disgusted voice, she said, "My husband and I are going to sue you for endangering minors. You are a disgusting, vulgar man, who is not fit to be teaching our precious, innocent children. You might not be losing your job today, thanks to the Alliance of Teachers, but we are going to make sure that every family at Dugwood knows how sickening you truly are."

When she called me "sickening," I was done. I had heard enough. I walked towards the door, then, at a good clip, intent on forcing the woman to back out of my way or be run down. I expected her to storm off as soon as she saw me approaching. But she didn't. She really didn't. That waif of a mother tried to stop me—all two-hundred-and-fifity-ish pounds of me!—from leaving my own classroom. What an insane idea. She couldn't win, so I grabbed her by the waist, picked up her rigid, ninety-pound, skin-and-bones body, and moved her out of my way. I deposited her, in her white leather coat, pink-faced and speech-less in the hallway outside my classroom, and went home.

That evening, over beer at a trendy new pub that had just opened in my neighbourhood, I told James the story about Mrs. Peach.

"I can't believe you said that to a parent," said James, dabbing the corners of his eyes with a napkin, his blue-rimmed glasses propped on his forehead. "Did you really pick her up?"

"Yes, I did," I said, hoisting a beer in my own honour.

"Can you really pass gas on demand?" James was laughing so hard, he snorted.

"Of course. Can't you?" I said matter-of-factly. "Can't all men?"

"I don't know," he said, sucking a piece of chicken out of his braces. "I've never tried, not since I was eight, anyway."

"Insanity. The hyper-helicopter protectionism, the screen time. It's not real, not honest. It's backwards, or upside-down, or something like that. You don't raise kids that way, sheltering them from everything except video games. All the wrong things are being taught in all the wrong ways. We're raising idiots. Do you get what I'm saying? Why can't teachers tell a story or fart in class?"

James was howling. Well-dressed customers at nearby tables looked over at us. He took his blue-rimmed glasses off his fore-head and tossed them on the table, so that he could wipe away more tears of laughter.

Once he recovered himself, and put his glasses back on, James said to me with half-seriousness, "I think they call it a mid-life crisis."

I couldn't help chuckling at that. He wasn't right, but it was funny. Following my lead, we raised our glasses and drank to every man who had, was, or would be going through one of those.

"Funny," I said, "I was sure I had mine when I heaved Cindy and her pepperoni pizza out the backdoor. This is different, though. I don't know what's wrong with me."

James looked at me straight in the eyes. "When's the last time you had a date?"

"College," I said, not having to think very hard about it. Cindy was the last woman I dated.

James was wide-eyed and smiling, "No...seriously, can't be. How long ago was that?"

"1986...same year I bought my car."

"What about after your divorce?"

"No one."

"Not even a kindergarten teacher?"

"No."

The waitress came over, and James ordered me another drink, even though I still had half a glass left. Then he lowered that soft chin of his and looked over his nose at me. "Really, Beast? That can't be right. Are you sure?"

"I haven't dated anyone since Cindy," I said, putting my right hand on my heart. "I swear on...my mother's life."

"Why not?"

"I need to sell my house first."

James squinted at me, apparently not buying my logic. "What does a house have to do with dating?"

"Everything—nothing. I don't know."

"That's all you've got, master storyteller—a shrug and 'I don't know'?"

I shrugged again and glanced around.

James put his beer down and put his hands up on either side of his face. "Look at me, Harry."

I did.

"Would you just ask her out!"

I shrugged again and looked over at a table where a couple, about my age, was holding hands.

"Or are you that worried she'll shoot you down?"

"Who?" I said, though I knew exactly who he was talking about.

"I could punch you right now," he said.

Neither of us spoke for a moment.

We drank.

James leaned across the table. He was tight-faced but friendly, like a counsellor who really believes he can reach into someone's soul and bring it out into the world for a quick repair. "You know," he said, his tone kinder, "the other day, you said something about a quote: 'Those who tell the stories rule society.' Who said that?"

"Plato. I got it from the side of a coffee mug. Marigold Lovitt's daughter sent it to her from university. The kid's finished her first novel already, and she's barely out of diapers."

"Why don't you take Plato's advice then? He was a smart guy. Tell yourself a happy, upbeat story like: boy meets girl, boy is scared, boy overcomes fear, boy gets girl, and they live happily ever after. You can tell your own story. And it can be a good one, as good and as happy as you want it to be."

If James thought I was reachable that night, he was wrong; I was getting drunk, not getting therapy.

"The only one making you miserable, Harry Tyke," he pronounced as he leaned away from me and picked up his glass, "is Harry Tyke."

"Do you really think I'm in her league?"

"Olga's?"

"Yes, Olga's," I insisted.

James almost spat out his beer as he stifled a laugh. "No way! You're not even close. But you never know. Maybe she's into fuzzy, grade-six teachers nicknamed Beast who are having a midlife crisis and want to suddenly take on the Education Agency and save us all from raising more idiots."

I hoisted my glass and drained it.

"You never know," I repeated on the heels of a satisfying belch. "Maybe I'm not that bad."

James raised his glass. I raised the fresh full one, which the waitress had just placed on a coaster in front of me.

"Maybe you're not that bad, Beast," he said.

Several hours, several drinks and a taxi ride later, I was home. The first thing I did when I got inside was go down to my fart room and let one rip for Mrs. Peach. Drunkenly satisfied, I went upstairs and sat down in my office without turning on any lights. The light coming from the computer monitor wasn't quite the same as a long, white candle in a brass candlestick, but it was all I could manage at the moment.

Dear Olga, I typed. *I would like to respectfully ask you to go on a naked date with me. Harry Tyke.* Without hesitation, I pressed send. Then I leaned back and stared at Olga's picture on my computer monitor until the image started to spin and swim, and I had to close my eyes.

The garbage truck pulled up in the alley the next morning and woke me up. My mouth was dry, and I urgently had to go to the bathroom. I wanted to go down to my fart room first, but I didn't have the energy nor the coordination to negotiate stairs, nor did I have the time. I had ten minutes to get to school.

I was out the door and starting the car in less than five minutes, unshaven and wearing the same clothes I had slept in, which now smelled faintly like pepperoni pizza. I backed out of the driveway with a screech, and just as I shifted into first gear, I remembered the email. In a fresh panic, I pulled back into the driveway, jogged up the front steps, unlocked the door and bolted to my office.

I sat down and jiggled the mouse. The computer was frozen. A host of updates had downloaded during the night, so rebooting took much longer than usual. I ate a piece of toast, drank three glasses of water, took a two-minute shower, and changed my clothes. The computer was just finishing its reboot when I sat down at my desk again. I clicked my way to my email inbox as quickly as the machine would allow, but the Internet connection was slow. I leaned way back in my chair as I waited for the inbox to open. There it was—Olga's reply. I chewed at my whiskers. I wanted to know what her answer was. I didn't want to know what her answer was. I felt ill from drinking three big glasses of water so quickly. I grabbed my keys and went down to my fart room. I lit one up for Cindy and Mr. Chicago—me versus the pepperoni. I went to school. Teaching was a hell that I could cope with, a rejection from Olga was not.

I was very late arriving at Dugwood. Otto Logan's special needs assistant was babysitting my class. I had to look at Otto twice before I realized the boy had shoulder pads stitched under the fabric of his orange t-shirt. The students were quiet when I walked in. I asked them to pull their desks into a circle and take off their shoes. I asked Alexa to turn off the lights and pull down the blinds. In my rush out the door, I had forgotten to bring a candle from home.

"Well," I said, when Alexa was back in her desk, "after lunch you have the online safety test, and I think the best way to get you ready is to turn the studying over to you."

The students groaned.

"Let me finish," I said. "Forget about writing this stuff down. Forget about a quiz. We're going to hear your true, personal stories about being online. But first, you need to warm up—your voices and your bodies."

The students snickered and looked at each other. Unperturbed, I took them through two exercises that Olga had done in her workshop. First, I had them go around the circle and say their names out loud in a funny, exaggerated, expressive way, just like I had with the word mortgage. I encouraged them to applaud each other, and to laugh out loud, and to be okay with being silly. Then I had them stand up inside the circle made by their desks and pretend to be animals with their bodies. They were bears. They were ants. They were whales. They were wolves, and they said together in a wolf's growly voice, "I'll huff and I'll puff and I'll blow your house down!" Then I had them sit down again. I asked them to close their eyes and imagine a time when something went wrong with the computer. I gave them a moment to recall that memory. Then I had them tell it to a partner. After that vigorous warm up, I asked for volunteers to stand up in the middle of the circle and share their stories with the class. Alexa wanted to go first.

She brushed her long, black hair out of her eyes and stood up pin straight. Alexa was playing her mother, and she went straight into character, saying: "You can't play social games anymore, Alexa. I don't want you meeting questionable strangers on the computer." Alexa had her hands on her hips and wiggled them while she imitated her mother's voice. Then she switched back to her regular voice and body and said, "But, Mom, I have real friends online. I can't just vanish. They'll miss me." She went back and forth between her own voice and body and her mother's, so that it felt like we had actually witnessed their conversation.

When Alexa finished, I asked her where this had happened. She said she had been sitting on her bed with her tablet when her mom had come in and started in on her. I asked her about the colour of her bedding, and whether or not her bed was made, and if there were any background sounds, and what time of day it was. As Alexa filled in the details, other students started to raise their hands, eager to tell their stories, too.

Polly, a shy, intelligent student who rarely participated in class, had her arm ramrod straight in the air. I told Polly that she could be the next storyteller, after Tyler—who had raised his arm a split second before she had—then I asked the class, "How old do you have to be to have your own social media account?"

"Thirteen," came the reply, all at once, from the entire class.

"Do you think it's smart to be online friends with people you have never met in real life?" No one raised their hand. "Do you?" I repeated.

Otto Logan put his hand up and answered, "My dad says online friends are the best. He's on the computer all the time. He plays really late at night when he gets home from his gigs at the comedy club. Mom gets really mad about it. She makes him go to bed. And one time my dad got so mad about it that he threw the mouse at her, and it hit her in the head. I didn't see it, but I heard it. My room is right next to my dad's office."

Tyler went next. "My mom plays online games with a bunch of people. She puts her headset on and games out, and my little sister and I don't get dinner until really late when my dad gets home from work, unless I make it. Sometimes I make dinner earlier because my sister is hungry, and I make a plate for my mom and put it in front of her while she's gaming. Sometimes she eats it. Yeah." Tyler wiped at his eyes with the sleeve of his t-shirt. "But…most of the time the food just gets cold, and then she throws it in the garbage. She tells my dad that she only plays for one hour. But that's not true. She tells me and my sister to go play our own games in the family room. We're getting sick of it, so we mostly go outside and ride our bikes. But my mom doesn't like that. She says playing video games is safer than riding our bikes. At least in video games you can't really get hurt. That's what she says."

And around the room it went for an hour. When the recess bell interrupted us, I promised to tell them a funny little detail from my own story when they came back in. The students, though, didn't care about recess. They wanted to hear the little detail right away. So, without making them beg too much, I told them about my fart room; and in the spirit of using your voice and body to tell a good story, I let a rib-shaking fart rip through my rear end and explode into the classroom. The students loved it, but they bolted outside immediately, thankful it was still recess. I can't blame them. I went down to the staffroom to get a cup of coffee.

7

Dear Olga. I would like to respectfully ask you to go on a naked date with me. Harry Tyke.

It was after midnight, and for the fifth time that evening, I stared at the unopened reply from Olga. After school, I had kept myself busy, busier than I had been in a long time. I was exhausted and my arms and shoulders were killing me, but it was a good exhaustion—physical, not just mental. Feeling like a man of action, like a man with new hope for a better future, I had decided two blocks from home that I was going to update the house to get it ready for sale. I didn't need it. It was time to move on, time to get rid of this oversized liability, this anchor around my neck. As soon as I had walked in the front door after school, I dropped my trench coat, took off my sweater vest and shirt, and threw myself into tearing up the green shag carpet in the living room. By eight o'clock, I had the living room and dining room furniture stored in my old bedroom upstairs and the floor stripped bare to the carpet nails and floor boards.

Craving more, I had gone to the nearest hardware store and bought myself a six-pound sledgehammer and a pair of leather gloves. I had walked up to the till with no gloves and a twenty-pound hammer, but then a broad-shouldered tradesman, almost my height, who was in line in front of me, politely suggested that I go with the lighter hammer and a pair of gloves. He said that twenty-pound sledges were for gorillas and murderers, not hardworking men such as ourselves. I said, "What about beasts?" And he had laughed and said, "Not even big, hairy ones like us," by which he really meant me, because the guy had a perfectly clean-shaven face, even though it was after eight. Regardless of his poking fun at my beard, I trusted his advice and came home with the six-pounder and the gloves and demolished the brick fireplace.

The computer chimed at me. I had a new Friendzone message. It was a friend request from my ex-wife, Cindy. I never checked Friendzone, so it took me a few minutes to remember what my three regular passwords were and which one would let me in. Once in, I scanned the page thinking Olga might be on there. I ignored Cindy's request and typed in Olga's first and last name and hit the search button. Olga's face popped up, so did her relationship status: single. Somehow, it would have been easier if she was married or in a relationship. Then I could have admired her from a distance and daydreamed about her safely from afar, like a fan or groupie.

Instead of opening Olga's reply to my drunken, naked date request, I assumed it was a no, and decided that a long, hot bath would help my aching body recover from all that glorious manual labour. I winced when I picked up my sledgehammer, my new companion. Blisters were coming up on my palms, despite the gloves. Gingerly, I carried the hammer to the bathroom, and leaned it up against the side of the toilet.

In the tub, I tried to focus one hundred percent of my thoughts on everything except Olga. What did I really need to do to get the house ready for sale? When it sold, where would I move to? Should I go to Cuba? I'd love to go there. Could I? What would I do for work if I left the country? If I stayed, would I keep teaching? What about writing? Was I going to write a book someday? Could I earn my living as a writer? Was it too late to go back to being a copy editor? I wonder what that email says? I rubbed my whiskers with my wet hands.

"What do you think?" I said aloud to my sledgehammer.

Knowing the answer, I got out of the tub, leaving the towels on the floor where they had been since my last bath, and walked, dripping, downstairs to the main floor and down the hallway to the office. I sat my wet body down in the leather office chair, letting the water pool around my thighs, and opened the message from Olga. It said:

Yes, Harry. I will go on a naked date with you. It sounds fun. Please let me know when and where. Call me. Olga. She had put her phone number beneath her name.

I had assumed it would be a no; I had not prepared for a yes. So I did nothing.

The next day, in the afternoon, I was counting heads. "Olga, two, three, four. Olga, two, three, four," I said aloud as I numbered the students off into small groups. Even though it was Friday afternoon, and I was looking forward to spending the weekend with my sledgehammer, it had not been a good day. I hadn't called Olga yet and hated myself for being such a coward. On top of that, we had had a noon-hour visit from our union rep. Every teacher in the school had crammed into the staffroom to listen to an impassioned speech about how we were starting job action after spring break to protest the Education Agency's Bill 1010, which, if passed, would allow school districts to replace retiring teachers with a new Educational Digital Delivery System (EDDS) and education assistants, rather than hire new teachers. According to the Delegate for Education, the government's goal was to have fifty percent of all teaching delivered through EDDS by 2020. Apparently, the recent need for a district-wide test on Internet safety was part of the contract that the Education Agency had already signed with the company delivering EDDS. The teachers were up in arms about all this, not because they disagreed with the principles of digitally delivered education, but because they were worried about losing their jobs. They argued that a fully-qualified teacher needed to be in the classroom in order for EDDS to be effective, and that the government had no right to kill an entire profession.

My colleagues, even James, were frothing by the end of the union rep's impassioned speech. Before we adjourned, we voted—all in favour, save one abstainer—to begin job action immediately by going on classroom-only status and increasing the amount of curriculum delivered by computer by one hour per day, to demonstrate that teachers were necessary for a digital education program to be effective and legitimate. The only teacher to abstain from the vote was myself, of course. Despite the looks of horror around the room, I would not support a plan that put students in front of computers more than they already were. I just could not do it.

After the meeting, I decided not to follow my usual lesson plan. I was determined to give my students the naked classroom experience, just like Olga had in Mexico. It would give she and I something to talk about on our date, if I got up the nerve to call her. And with the union voting to add more computer time to the school day, I felt I needed to make a point. Forget computers. Forget cluttered classrooms. I was going to give the kids complete storytelling freedom in an open, empty space, no distractions, just us—our lovely selves.

"Olga, two, three, four. Olga, two, three, four," I continued until the students were divided into small groups. "Put your coats on, please. We are going outside to the undercover play area."

But the students had just come in from lunch, and they were cold. It was hovering around freezing outside, and, in a blizzard of cheeky comments, the protest quickly went from audible to obnoxious:

"It's snowing, Mr. Tyke."

"It's too cold, Mr. Tyke."

"That's a dumb idea, Beast."

"Yeah. We'll freeze our privates off."

"You don't have any privates, loser!"

"Do so!"

"Do not."

"How would you know, pervert?"

"Can't we have some computer time?"

"Yeah! Computer time."

"C'mon, Beast, computer time."

And then it started:

"Com-pu-ter-time! Com-pu-ter-time! Com-pu-ter-time!" it went, growing louder with each repetition, every little mouth in the room committed to grinding me down so that I'd give them what they wanted.

"Stop!" I shouted.

"Com-pu-ter-time!" they shouted back.

I sliced my hand across my throat and shouted at them to cease and desist.

They raised the volume and kept chanting.

I imagined the feel of my sledgehammer in my raw hands. I wished I had brought it up with me, for show and tell. But I hadn't. It was downstairs, in the teacher parking lot, in the back of my Horizon.

"Com-pu-ter-time!"

Sledgehammer-less as I was, I picked up the wooden stool and slammed it against the whiteboard. It exploded on impact in a shower of sticks; the seat flew off straight at Otto's head. Luckily, he was paying attention. He ducked just in time.

"Okay," I said, calmly picking a splinter of wood off my sweater vest. "If we can't get away from all this stuff," I gestured at the entire room, "then we are going to get the stuff away from us. Everyone pick up a piece of furniture—desks, shelves, pens, books, the computer, everything—and carry it out into the hall. Stack it neatly. Keep a pathway to our door."

The students obeyed very quickly, but they whispered their worries to each other as they moved every last bit of furniture out into the hallway and piled it up against their lockers. I used my running shoe to sweep up the bits and pieces of broken stool into a pile in a corner. Once the students were back inside what was now our "naked" classroom, I closed the door, turned off the lights and told them to sit on the floor in their small groups.

"Right. I apologize for losing my temper—screw it!—no, I don't. You kids had it coming."

None of them were whispering any more.

"Now, class, more than once you've seen and heard me tell my story; and you've had chances yourselves to tell each other stories about gaming, the online world and your crazy families; and you have practiced using your voices and bodies to tell stories; now it's time for you to put this all together in your underused brains and tell a story together as a group. I want each group to decide on a main character, give him or her a name and age, and choose a problem that this person could have—not a huge problem, we're not telling feature-length films here. We don't have that kind of time, so choose something small, a little problem…like a teacher who has just lost his job." I smiled at them. "Once you have your character, pick a setting. When you are ready, start passing your story around the circle. Everyone builds on the part that is passed to them. If the story comes to you and your brain blanks out, add some description. Any questions? No? Good. Go!"

They just looked at me.

"Go!" I commanded.

The students turned to their groups and started making up their stories. I was pleased by the thick hum in the room. Like Olga, I did not join a group. Instead, I floated around to get a taste of each group's story. Outside, snow started to whiten up the fields and playgrounds. Inside, in my naked classroom, I started to notice a theme in the stories—suicide. Most of the groups had a protagonist who was either bullied or neglected, and their story problem was whether or not the protagonist should commit suicide.

A while later, as I was telling the students to give their stories a title, Principal Caulfeild jerked the classroom door open and told me to get into the hallway. His face was purple above his stiff white collar and navy necktie.

I addressed Caulfeild from where I was kneeling in the middle of the room. "Anything you have to say to me, you can say in front of my students," I said.

He shook his head.

So I got up and went out into the hallway in my socks, leaving the door open.

He reached around me and closed the door. "What are you doing in there, Tyke?" he said.

"Renovations," I said, proudly. "We're redesigning our classroom to prove—"

"You have fifteen minutes to get this stuff back in the classroom. And I'm going to stand right here and make sure you do it."

Caulfeild opened the door and led me back into the classroom. He stopped short, took one look at the smashed stool and said, "Mr. Tyke, I must ask you to leave the school grounds, immediately."

I drove home with my window wide open and the heater on full blast. Now I really had a bond with Olga, something great to tell her: an amazing story about how I tried out her naked classroom as a protest against Bill 1010 and got expelled on mental health leave. I was going to call her the second I got home. I was going to set up a date for that night. Any time, any place she wanted. I was ready.

I called and left a long, wordy, excited message. I called again an hour later and left another equally wordy but more frustrated message. I called again. And again. My messages getting longer and more panicky. My sledgehammer and I smashed out the wall between the living room and dining room. And she didn't call me back. I gutted the 1967 kitchen. And she didn't call me back. With a single blow I took down the cuckoo clock from Zurich. And she still didn't call me back. I built a pile of rubble on my front lawn, causing an uproar with the neighbours. And still, she didn't call.

PART TWO

1

I sat across from James at my favourite spot in Positano, Italy—Ristorante Grotto d'Oro. My poor friend was still green and shaking from the drive from the Naples airport— along the hairpin highway that hugged the cliffside above the Mediterranean—to Positano, where I had been hanging out and hiding out for three weeks. I loved my little 1972 Fiat 500, with the scuffed side panels and dented bumpers, and got a kick out of giving the Italians a good run for their money on the narrow roads. But, poor James, I kickstarted his spring break junket with a two-hour drive unlike anything he had ever experienced in his tender life. As I dodged and swayed from Naples to Positano, the poor kid hadn't known whether to vomit or laugh. As soon as he saw it in the airport parking lot, he had called my little Fiat a clown car. I barely fit, despite the generous sag in the driver's seat, but I liked that when I threw my weight into the corners the whole car went with me.

I ordered a dish of olives, a plate of fresh cheese and a local citrus liqueur called Limoncello, which I thought might settle my friend's stomach. It was busy in the restaurant as most of the townsfolk were enjoying their drawn-out midday meal. We sat by an open window that overlooked the narrow bay and the town square with its seventeenth-century, beach-side cathedral. The rain had eased off to a drizzle, but it still felt more like mid-winter than early spring.

After a long, queasy silence, James said, "I can't believe you talked me into this."

I shrugged. "It's not so bad."

"I thought your secret fantasy was to be a Cuban fisherman like Hemingway." He zipped up his jacket and sniffed at the strong lemon beverage that had been placed in front of him by the waiter, who was now turning on the nearest floor heater. "This definitely isn't Cuba. There's better weather at home right now." James sipped the Limoncello, made a face and put the glass down on the linen table cloth. "Nasty. Worse than your driving."

"What are you talking about?" I smiled. It occurred to me that in my weeks away, I had missed his congenial harassment. "I'm a genius in my Fiat 500."

James put down his Limoncello and was delicately taking small sips from a bottle of sparkling water. Between sips, he said, "If Caulfeild finds out I'm here with you, he'll probably fire me too."

"Don't be so dramatic," I said, spitting an olive pit into my fingers. "They don't fire by association. Besides, I haven't been fired…yet," I laughed. "You didn't smash a stool against a white-board and try out my naked classroom trick, did you?"

James tried another sip of the liqueur and winced. "How do you meet girls in this place with all those stairs? Seems like it would be a bit of a pain. I haven't even seen any other tourists. Talk about the off season. This place is dead."

"Everyone arrives in a couple of weeks for Easter. It's been mostly the locals getting ready for the season and the odd tourist, and the roosters of course, but mainly I've been alone and writing, here or in my apartment."

James looked at me quizzically and took another sip of water. "What are you working on?"

"A book," I said, feeling very pleased with myself.

"A book? Like a novel?"

I shook my head and launched, very eagerly, into an explanation. I wanted to show off what I'd done. "A book about why the education system isn't working and why we need to start incorporating the old ways of teaching. I mean, the old, proven ways of teaching through dialogue and storytelling. That's why I'm here. I thought about Cuba, really thought about it, but I was craving the Old World—tradition, slowness, sanity…you know what I mean…I don't want to be in the New World anymore. The New World has our kids zoning out in front of screens, disconnected from their senses, their voices, their bodies—it's no great surprise that zombies are so central to popular culture—"

"Old World? There's nothing really that different here in Italy. It looks the same to me."

I shot back my Limoncello and banged the glass down on the table. "Perhaps not now…not so much. But there is a closeness here with the past that we don't have on the west coast of Canada. That's why I came here. Hemingway went to Cuba. I came to Positano. It's a simpler, more traditional life, closer to the soul…"

I could see he wasn't listening to me. James was looking out the window at the grey water and empty beach below, the sand dotted with upturned fishing boats.

"I know Positano isn't primitive," I continued. "I've got TV and Wi-Fi in my apartment, but there are opportunities, ancient places I went to in Rome, Ostia and Pompeii, where a man can stop and grapple with radically different times—times before computers and televisions and cell phones and tablets and books—times when learning was a human-to-human endeavour, not a human-to-machine-to-human one."

"So this isn't about Olga, then?" James said, flatly, without looking at me.

I motioned to the waiter to bring me the bill.

"Olga who?" I retorted, just as flatly.

James picked up a green olive and studied it and me at the same time. "So what's the state of the renovations? When can you move back in?"

I pulled out my wallet and paid. I wasn't interested in talking about home. That would require wine. "Let's get you set up," I said. We're driving back up the coast to Pompeii tomorrow." I held out the almost-full glass of Limoncello for him to finish.

James groaned and waved it away. "I need a beer, something normal. I don't think I can do all this foreign adventure stuff like you can. I'm about ready to get you to take me back to the airport so that I can go somewhere decent for vacation, somewhere there aren't crazy roads, crazy drivers and all these stairs, somewhere hot, where the girls are all in bikinis."

"I've got a fridge full of beer, just for you," I said, knowing James wasn't going anywhere. Just to tick him off, I added, "And, by the way, the women here are ladies not girls in bikinis. They're not going to mingle with skinny Canadian teachers with braces and blue glasses who can't drink a shot of Limoncello."

"Funny, Beast, how you forgot to tell me that on the phone."

"Funny."

"I swear this is about Olga," he said as he followed me out into the drizzle.

Passing me, James walked across the narrow shelf-of-a-road and squeezed between two parked cars to get a better look at the sea. "I wish you would just get this Olga thing out of your system," he said as he looked over the cliff.

"It's not about her," I said as I waited for him by the stairs.

James turned away from the view and crossed back over to where I was standing. "I have some news from home for you, good news."

I shrugged and started climbing up the one hundred irregular steps that led to my vacation apartment.

James called up from the bottom, "I don't feel like telling you this since I see you've dragged me to Hades for spring break."

"So don't tell me." I started climbing faster.

James shouted up at me, still at bottom, "You'll want to hear this."

I called over my shoulder, "Save it." I was starting to feel winded.

"It's about Olga," said James, jogging up behind me, effortlessly. He was right on my heels.

I started taking two steps at a time so that he wouldn't pass me.

"Did you hear me? It's about Olga."

We were halfway up to the apartment, and I was really starting to puff, so I stopped climbing and leaned on the chipped and stained plaster wall of someone's home. My thighs were tingling and I was really short of breath, but I tried to mask it. I faced James.

"What, then?"

It started to rain heavily. James grinned. He wasn't puffing at all, and I was jealous. It had taken me three weeks to be able to get this far up the stairs without feeling like I was going to pass out.

"Relax. It's good news."

"So tell me!"

He grinned. "I ran into her at the airport. She was seeing off some guy," said James, taking his glasses off to dry them on his t-shirt. "I don't know who it was, but it doesn't matter. She said she wants you to get in touch with her."

I shook my head with disbelief and tried to speak without giving away how winded I was. "Not possible. She didn't return any of my calls."

"Harry!" James said, emphatically putting his glasses back on. "She just got back from a three-week storytelling tour of Central America. She got your five messages the day before she bumped into me at the airport and was happy to know you were on a trip but disappointed that she missed you. She looked great. She had those red heels on again and looked—"

"She said that—those exact words?"

"Yeah, something like that. She said to give you a hug—which I won't—and she said to tell you that if you can get online you should send her an email. The guy she was seeing off looked choked when she mentioned you. So there you go! You're not so bad. We've got proof."

Standing there fifty steps above the street and fifty steps below my front door, I was frozen; my mind was both hyperactive and paralyzed. Did I really still have a chance with the most beautiful woman in the world?

James watched me process all this for a moment. Then he slapped me hard on the back and started up the stairs, jogging ahead of me. "Come on, Beast. This is good news, and by the way, all these stairs have been good for you. You've dropped a few pounds, eh? Next, maybe you'll lose that bramble nest on your face. You'll be ready for the naked storyteller when you get home—and I'll bet those New World conveniences like Wi-Fi and email are looking pretty good now, aren't they?"

I got my trembling legs moving again and puffed up the stairs, calling out to James who had finally stopped talking but had already run past my front door.

My apartment in Positano had three rooms—a kitchen, a sitting room with a foldout sofa where James slept, and a bedroom—all connected by windowless hallway which ran along the interior, cliffside wall of the apartment. The floors were laid with bright, colourful mosaic tiles, the walls were white and tastefully decorated with original seascapes, the furniture was a combination of modern and antique, the tiled kitchen was nicely set up with a six-burner gas stove, and every room gave me a spectacular view of the Mediterranean. A wide veranda ran across the sea side of the apartment, and each room had a set of glass double-doors leading out to it. It wasn't big, but it was much more a home than my giant house in Kerrisdale had ever been. I felt I could be myself in a new, stripped-down way. Its practical simplicity was good for my creative side too. I had written more than half my book in three weeks.

James had already stripped and was stepping into the shower off my bedroom by the time I got up to the apartment. His clothes were on my bed.

"Great view, Beast," he called from the bathroom when I came in. "I like your writing spot."

In the absence of a proper desk, I had brought in the patio table from the deck and set it up in my bedroom by the veranda doors. On the tiled table top was my laptop, two bottles of wine—one almost finished and the other still corked—and a bulbous, empty wine glass.

"That's my bathroom," I told James. "Yours is off the hallway."

"Sorry, Beast," called James.

I smiled, knowing he wasn't, and sat down at my desk, poured myself a full glass of wine and turned on my laptop.

"Are you going to send Olga an email?"

I wanted to, but I didn't know what to write. I took a long drink and held some of the tangy wine in my mouth as I looked out at the afternoon view. I loved the view, how it was the same every day. I saw the same stacks of pink and tan apartments set into the lush, often soggy, shrubs and stocky ornamental trees that grew out of the jagged brown cliffs. I saw the same puffed, grey rain clouds, the same mist over the sea, the same thin swath of car-lined concrete winding down the hill towards the beach, the same construction site in the little grotto in the curve in the road. I saw the same lonely lemon tree rising out of the garden of the last house at the end of the peninsula, the same grey sea beyond it. The setting didn't change. It was summer beauty over-cast by late-winter grunge wrapped in a rainy sheen; and I was at home on the cliffside in the rain with my laptop and my bottles of Italian wine. In Positano, I had been as happy as I could imagine being, ever. But now that a relationship with Olga was a possibility again, I ached to see this same view in the summer in its full glory, with blue skies instead of puffy, grey clouds. I ached to feel the sizzling Amalfi sun on my body as I lay nearly naked on the veranda. Rainy, late-winter Positano wasn't as homy now that the longings for Olga were back at the front of my thoughts. I wanted summer and heat. I wanted sunshine and Olga in a red bikini.

I got up and turned the heat up a few degrees. James came out of the bathroom with a towel wrapped around his thin, muscular waist. Seeing him shirtless made me wonder why James and Olga really hadn't gone on a second date.

2

"The naked storyteller would love this place," James said, smiling at a two-thousand-year-old fresco of a robust, suntanned Roman, who held a pink-skinned woman with protruding breasts in his muscular arms.

After a drunken rainy night, we walked the rocky streets of ancient Pompeii under a clear blue sky. All day James had been pointing out erotic art on the ancient walls and making allusions to Olga—and my desire for her. The teasing was starting to grate on my nerves.

On our way out, James stopped at a street vendor's stall and bought a postcard, which had sixteen different erotic scenes on it. "I'm going to send this to Olga and say it's from you," he said, waving the postcard in my face.

I chose to ignore him.

We were soon back at the car, which I had parked in a lot that was also an orange grove. While he was waiting for me to unlock the door, James jumped up and grabbed an orange from one of the smaller trees. "You just have to pick her, like an orange," he explained to me as if he was the mentor and I a lowly student of love. "She's already said she'd go out with you, and now you're here in Pompeii wandering empty streets, looking at ancient pornographic art, drinking too much, and writing a book that six people will read, while at this very moment there is an absolutely gorgeous woman back in Vancouver who wants to go out with you—one who you obviously can't get off your mind. I heard you tossing and groaning last night. You want her. You're just too afraid to do anything about it."

I grabbed the orange and ripped the postcard out of James's hand. I threw the orange into the bushes, tore up the postcard and shoved the bits of stiff paper in my pocket. Pointing at him over the roof of my Fiat 500, I said, "You're the one who can't get her off your mind. You're the one who has been talking about her non-stop today. You're the one who needs another date with her. Not me!"

James put his hands up as if to surrender. "Listen. I'm sorry I've been bugging you all day. It's just that I'm…not jealous… well, maybe I am…I mean, she wants you!" he snapped. His face going red.

"That's not my fault," I said, backing down.

James looked genuinely distressed and hesitated a bit at first before explaining why he had been teasing me more than usual.

I waited for him, leaning on the roof of my car in that orange grove, patiently waiting for my young friend to put his story together.

James sighed. "We had this really nice date. We went out for a nice dinner downtown and then for a walk on Robson Street. Nothing happened. We didn't even hold hands or anything, but we had fun, and then I didn't call her because nothing happened; and I was surprised because I'm an attractive guy, and I think she's attractive, but she wasn't feeling it. I could tell she wasn't feeling it. So embarrassing. That's the first time in my life I've been on a date where the woman didn't want to jump me. She acted more like I was her little brother than her date. That doesn't happen to me, and I still think she's hot, but, really, if she likes a guy like you then—I know when to move over. She's not a cougar, apparently. She likes older guys, grizzly, old guys like you with armpit stains and beer bellies who can't jog up a flight of stairs without getting into heart attack territory. I bought her a nice dinner, too, a really nice dinner, but she wasn't into me. It was weird. I mean, she's into you, Harry. She wants you. She told me to give you a hug. Do you get me? Stuff like that doesn't happen every day."

I looked at James and, in thought only, added, "No kidding. It's a flipping miracle."

Having finished his confession, James stood quietly, waiting for me to get in the car.

He shook his head mockingly at me as he watched me squeeze into the driver's seat. He hopped in beside me, his mood lighter, chuckling.

"What were you thinking when you bought this thing?"

I started the car and shrugged, my head grazing the roof. "It was parked on the side of the road in Rome, and it looked cheap and easy to drive. I only paid a couple hundred euros for it, and it's good for these narrow highways. Besides, it's fun driving stick shift again. Takes me back to my youth."

"I've never driven stick before."

"Big surprise," I said, feeling disarmed for the first time that day. "No wonder a real woman like Olga doesn't want a young buck like you. You can't even drive stick. Maybe I'll give you a lesson while you're here."

I swung us around a tight corner to avoid hitting a bus.

"No, thanks, you old beast," said James, hanging on to the dash. He winced as we missed the corner of a building by a finger width. "You couldn't pay me a million dollars to drive this clown car. I'd like to go home alive. I've got women to date, young Canadians who dig skinny teachers with blue glasses and braces."

We arrived back in Positano in the early evening. It was pleasant enough that I could sit outside on the veranda and write. James had gone out for dinner with Philomena, an

English-speaking Italian girl in her early twenties, who assisted the owner of the apartment. She happened to stop by at the same time we had arrived back from Pompeii. She wanted to see if I needed anything. As soon as the words "thank you, we are fine" came out of my mouth, James had successfully asked the young lady to be his "tour guide" for the evening and, poof, they were gone, leaving me alone on the veranda to come up with a dashing, manly, sweep-her-off-her-feet kind of email for Olga. It was harder than it sounded.

Looking back, I realize that I was fretting over nothing, but the truth is, that even with the layer of happiness I had found in that setting and in writing my first book, I didn't see my anxiety about the email as fretting over nothing. I was fretting over everything, my whole world, every layer of my being. So, instead of taking advantage of the peace and quiet of that lovely evening and using it as inspiration to write a dashing follow up to my "naked date" email, I opened my manuscript and wrote a few thousand words about education in ancient Pompeii, but it was just a bit of material about corporal discipline that I didn't find particularly gripping, so I actually did more drinking and staring out at the water than I did writing. Then, some hours and some wine later, bored with my book, I let the exotic romance of the barking dogs and crashing waves and car horns invade my senses, and my words, and I typed up a classic love letter. I felt it was almost Shakespearean and was deeply proud of it. I clicked the send button with deep confidence in myself as a man and a writer; then I raised my glass and toasted the sea to my future happiness and promptly passed out in my chair out on the veranda, under the overcast Positano sky.

I woke up the next morning, flat on my back on the bed with my laptop in my arms, hugged tight to my chest. I could hear James snoring in the sitting room. It was bright but cool outside. I made coffee and went out on the veranda. I felt celebratory. My love letter would sweep Olga off her feet. She would be so enamoured that she would hop the next plane to Naples. I would pick her up at the airport. She would be in her glossy red heels, looking fresh and happy. Her smile would brighten even more when she saw me. I would be in my best jeans and a nice Italian dress shirt, which I would buy the second I knew she was on her way. I would say, "*Ciao, bella!*" or something romantic like that. She would throw her arms around me, and we would kiss for such a long time it would make the Italians blush. Then, hand in hand, we would walk to my Fiat 500, and I would show her that I was master of the road, master of the entire length of the ancient, rugged Amalfi coast.

"Where's the coffee cream?" James asked from the kitchen door.

"There's a can of whipping cream in the fridge."

"That was quite an email you wrote last night," James yelled from the kitchen. "You didn't send that, did you? You'd never say that to a woman you've never dated, would you?" Wearing only his underwear, he came out with his coffee and stood at the railing next to me.

"You didn't read it, did you?"

"Women don't like that sort of thing, Beast. They like cool, mysterious, distant, not gushing love letters." James wrapped his arms around his taut, hairless chest. "It's cold out here."

"Everyone on that hill can see you."

James went through the patio doors directly into the sitting room. Through the wide-open doors, I watched him rummage through his suitcase. He came back out on the deck again wearing all black.

"Wish I'd brought my ski jacket," he said. "Actually, I wish you had picked marlin fishing in Cuba ... I bet it's warmer there, much warmer."

"I told you the ladies here don't just fall for some guy they just met, especially not some foreigner. Philomena's a nice girl. She's got some sense…and probably some very traditional parents whom she respects."

"Don't fret, Beast. I get another shot today. We're driving down to some grotto," he grinned at me, "and I'm taking her in your car."

My coffee went down the wrong pipe as I laughed. "To Smeraldo Grotto? That's ten kilometres of hairpins, and you don't drive stick!"

"I guess we have a project for the morning, then. She's coming over at noon."

"Really? You want to take her in the clown car?"

He shrugged. "That's the only car we've got."

"Yeah, sure, I'll teach you…" I couldn't stop myself from asking, "Do you really think my email was too much?"

"Yes, I do. It was way too much! I saw it when I put you to bed last night. What a sap you are. You might have scared her away for good. I can't that believe you—straight up!—told her that you are in love with her."

Worried now, I excused myself and took my coffee to the bedroom, where I set up my laptop up on my makeshift desk and waited to see what the damage was.

James tapped on the glass of the closed veranda door to my room. "You're freaking out aren't you?"

Not looking up, I said, "Not at all."

"C'mon, Beast, what did she say?"

I opened Olga's email. It said a lot of nice things about my decision to come to Italy and write a book, and that getting put on leave sounded not so bad, and that it was an opportunity I might end up being thankful for; then right at the end, in the last sentence, like a six-pound sledgehammer, no a twenty-pound sledgehammer, in my skull, she had written: *I truly look forward to getting to know you better as a friend.* After reading that sentence, I almost did two things: punch James in the face for stirring me up, and jump off the balcony and kill myself. But I didn't do either.

I took my young, skinny, hairless friend out for an old-school driving lesson.

After two hours, and despite my best effort, James couldn't seem to get the hang of shifting gears.

"Clutch. Gas. Easy. Clutch. Now more gas," I said, holding the dashboard with both hands to brace myself while the car lurched and jerked down the narrow, single lane highway. "School bus!"

James swerved, hit the brakes and bounced off the thin band of metal that stood between us and the cliff. I'd had enough.

"Just pull over!"

"What! Why?" said James. "I thought I had it there for a minute."

"Yes, a minute, but a minute is not going to get you and Philomena, safely, to the grotto."

"Are you sure?"

I nodded. "Even if you do get there alive, it's going to be a waste of time. I've driven down at least a dozen times, and, every time, the old guy with the boat tells me it's closed. A dozen times, he's pointed at the waves and said to me: *non possibile.*"

"Why not possible?"

"The bad weather and storms have made it too dangerous to take the boat across to the grotto. You'll see. It'll be the same for you today, if you can get down there by some other mode of transport. You're not driving this. You'll have to take her on the bus or rent scooters, maybe, if you think you can handle it."

"How about I tell her I want to go out for drinks in town or a walk on the beach?"

"Good idea, Romeo. Now get out and let me drive."

By the time I parked the car, and we were climbing the steps to the apartment door, the noon-hour cathedral bells had already rung and Philomena was sitting politely on the stairs with a shiny, quilted black ski jacket in her lap and a blue wool scarf wrapped loosely around her neck. Her long dark hair was pulled back in a no-nonsense ponytail. When she saw us coming, she stood up and smiled.

"We can't go to the grotto," James said right away. "I can't drive Harry's car. I tried, but—I'm sorry. It won't be safe for either of us. I don't know how to drive stick."

I was impressed by his honesty and got the impression he really liked this girl.

Philomena looked at me with a raised eyebrow.

"*Cambio manuale*," I said.

"*Manuale?*" echoed Philomena. "No problem."

I handed her the keys and wished them luck at the grotto, which, from looking at the sea, I knew would be closed with the old man's *non possibile*. But it didn't matter. Little things like closed grottos mean nothing when you are falling in love, and I could see very plainly that my friend was well on his way.

3

A week later, I was back home, still on mental health leave, and up to my armpits in renovations. Carlo, the contractor I had hired on a whim the day I arrived home, stood in the empty space between my kitchen and the dining room with a cigarette hanging out of his mouth giving me a lecture.

"You are a teacher, not builder. Trust me, Teacher, the wall must go back, right here." He waved his cigarette through the open space between us.

"But open concept is what sells," I argued. "You told me that yourself on the phone."

"Yes. But not for you. No possible."

No possible? I didn't like being reminded that the day James had taken Philomena to the Smeraldo Grotto that the old man hadn't in fact said *non possibile* and had instead taken them on a long, romantic tour of the grotto on relatively calm waters, whereas I left the Amalfi Coast without being able to see it. Happy as I was for my friend and his new romance, it irked me.

One of Carlo's assistants, a young man with a huge moustache and a bare chest under his coveralls, shook his head sadly, as if my missing wall was the worst thing he'd ever heard in his young life.

"Can't you reinforce the existing walls or do something with the ceiling? How about a pillar?" I asked. "Something Roman, maybe?"

"Yes. But no possible on your budget, Teacher. No possible."

"Fine," I said, "no possible."

I grabbed my keys and headed out the front door. I had my first appointment with the union-appointed psychologist that morning; and, despite the fact that I felt like I had been bleeding cash since I stepped off the plane, I was glad for an excuse to get out of the house and let Carlo and his crew work. The sooner they finished, and I could put the house on the market, the better.

An hour later, with renovations underway at home, I was sitting in a cheap lounge chair in the corner of the psychologist's office. He was a younger fellow, in his forties, with a puffy, pale face and tight curls, who felt justified charging me two hundred and fifty dollars an hour to have a conversation. Bargain furniture aside, it took me right back to the four-hundred-dollar-an-hour negotiations I had had with Cindy and our lawyers about who was going to get my house. I had once met an older fellow at Jitters—a minister, I think he said he was—who said to me: "Twenty-five lawyers at the bottom of a lake is a good start." I suspected the same was true of psychologists.

"What are you thinking about, Harry?" asked the psychologist. His name was Richard Petersen. He sat diagonally across from me in a much nicer, taller office chair with his back up against his corner desk. I sat in the opposite corner in that cheaper, lower chair that was staring to hurt my back. The room was empty between us, except for a cheap-looking, shaggy rug. I just looked at him.

"I see." Richard leaned back in his chair, put his fingertips together in front of his chest and smiled. "Well, Harry, why do you believe you are here?"

"My union rep gave me your number. I didn't really have a choice. I smashed a stool and emptied my classroom. I was put on stress leave. I went to Italy. I'm back. I can't afford an open concept reno on a house I hate and I..."

Richard picked up a file folder, put it in his lap and opened it. "You smashed a wooden stool and emptied out your classroom, it says here."

"I said that already." I had no intention of baring my soul to this junior quack. I wasn't going to tell him that I was secretly hoping to sell my house and get enough money for it that I could quit teaching to write. I adjusted my position in the cheap chair trying to relieve the stiffness in my back. It was killing me, and it had only been five minutes.

Taking charge of the conversation, I said, "You're a young buck. You're not married, evidently. Where's a good place to take a lady out on a date these days?"

The guy didn't skip a beat.

"I have a formula, Harry. It works every time," he said, closing the file folder and putting it back on his desk. "Do you want to know how I woo a woman? I won't charge your extra." He smiled.

"Of course."

He crossed his legs, revealing tired, brown socks sticking out of tired, brown loafers. "I invite her over for dinner. I have this routine: I bake a frozen lasagna, make a salad from a bag, open a bottle of red, then sit her down in a chair just like that one you are sitting in, and give her a foot massage. Whist I expertly rub her tired toes, I promise to treat her like a queen for the rest of her life. Works every time."

"This chair is killing my back. You'd think at your rate you'd be able to show a lady a good time on the town and buy a decent chair for her to sit in."

Richard wrinkled his nose as if I had just farted or said something hilariously incomprehensible. "Girls don't need a good time on the town to feel special. It's all in what you say and where you touch them. I call it the right touch and the right tone. The foot massage is the clincher."

I looked at him skeptically.

"I'm serious. You could serve dry bread crusts and water followed by a foot massage and sweet nothings, and you'd get lucky. Tell me about this beautiful someone you're interested in."

"She's perfect."

"Really? You've met the perfect girl—"

"Woman."

Richard picked up a pad of paper, made a note and slipped it in the file folder. "How do you think destroying your classroom fits into all of this?"

"Aren't you supposed to tell me how it all fits together?"

Richard sighed thoughtfully through his nose and put his pen up to his lips. A screen saver with an animated aquarium bubbled silently behind the psychologist's back. A yellow and red striped angel fish swam off the left edge of the screen and swam back on the right. It made me think about where I should take Olga for our first date—seafood at Kits Beach? I felt I should try to live up to my "naked date" idea, even though I still had no idea what that looked like in practice. She would be expecting a call. I hadn't even told her a time or where I was taking her. Since reading her email in Positano, I had been ruminating about the idea of just being friends with her. I didn't think I could do it and was clinging to the possibility that she had said it just to be ladylike. We had not corresponded much since I professed my love for her, other than to exchange casual pleasantries, largely about the weather, both in Vancouver and Positano. I had been worrying obsessively about screwing things up and wanted our first date to be perfect; I had to make her forget about this "friends" idea.

"You don't want to be here, Harry. Am I right?"

"Correct."

"I understand, but here's how it works with me and the union."

"Tell me, please," I said rolling my eyes. I had really had enough of this loser.

"A guy like you, Harry, a decent guy, he snaps. Maybe he's sick with some midlife illness like cancer or heart disease; maybe he's just tired of dealing with students; maybe it's an addiction problem or a relationship gone sideways. The exact issue is irrelevant. He's lost it. He gets put on mental health leave, and the union sends him for mandatory counselling, to me. If the guy does the recommended twenty sessions, he's usually back in the classroom within a few months, full pay, no problems, no questions asked. It's like it never happened. Except the guy has had a well-earned break, gets his emotions back under control..."

Twenty sessions with this guy? I could not imagine it, not unless I could bring my sledgehammer with me.

I said, "And if he doesn't cough up—let's see, five grand for these miracle sessions, then what?"

"Before you jump to any decisions, I want you to understand that early retirement can be tough, if you don't have a plan in place. You should at least give it a try. Do three or four sessions. We'll talk, man to man. I'll listen to your story. Maybe you'll figure some things out. We can start with something small, like where to take that girl of yours on a date."

"Woman," I corrected him.

"That's what I meant."

"I won't take up any more of your time, then," I said, ready to leave. I had to use both hands to hoist myself up out of the overly reclined, unsupportive chair.

"I would reconsider, Harry. Ask yourself: are you worth the money? I believe you are." He looked closely at me, pursing his lips. "Do you?"

I was on my way out, but at the door I stopped and added, "I won't be paying for today, by the way. You did nothing worth two hundred and fifty dollars."

Richard's face reddened as he looked up at me from the safety of his cushy chair. "Suit yourself, Harry. Good luck to you."

I almost made a comment about the shocking absence of luck in my life but didn't. Then I went to the parkade to discover my Horizon had been towed.

4

"No possible," said Carlo as he jogged down the front steps of my house to his truck.

I chased him to the sidewalk. "But you're the one who said I should take my date to your cousin's restaurant."

"This place is very popular. It is a taste of Italy, true Roman culture. She will love it. She will want to travel with you to Roma, or at least to your bedroom," Carlo grinned at me, then opened his truck and jumped inside.

I put my hands on the open window ledge so that he wouldn't drive away. "But my date is tomorrow night."

"Saturday night. Very busy. Booked for weeks, months!" said Carlo emphatically. "Wish I could help you, Teacher." He started his truck. "I see you Monday. We put wall back in house."

I finally got it. "You want money. I see. Okay. How much?"

"One hundred for five o'clock. Two hundred for eight o'clock," said Carlo, with a straight face.

"How much would it be if I wasn't already letting you gouge me on this reno?" I wanted to ask as I took out my wallet and counted out two hundred dollars.

Carlo took the bills and drove away shouting, "*Ciao*, Teacher! Good luck!"

I watched him drive away through the unbroken archway of hundred-foot elm trees. The weather office was calling for a nice weekend. If it was a nice evening, and things went well at dinner, I would suggest to Olga that we take an after-dinner walk, maybe at the beach.

When Carlo's truck turned the corner, I went back in the house and analyzed the mess: the plywood floors, the studs and drywall, the scraps of wood and dust in the corners, the ladders, tool boxes, and table saws. The entire main floor was out of commission. I was now living in the basement and had turned it into a bachelor apartment of sorts. It had a foldout sofa, bar, and full-size fridge that my parents had installed for hosting poker nights. It also had a small bathroom with a shower stall, and my fart room, of course. I always had the door to my fart room closed to keep the smell contained, but looking around at the dated furniture, wood-panel walls, and wobbly card table I was using as a desk, I knew I couldn't bring a woman like Olga over, not even if our date went really well, and she wanted to be more than friends.

I sat down at the card table and jiggled the mouse. I hadn't written a word in the week that I had been home from Italy. I still had more than a third of the book left to write, and, somewhere along the way, I had lost my drive to finish it. I found myself wondering what I was really going to do with it when it was finished. I doubted I would have the courage to send it to a publisher. I didn't even know how to do that. I had helped my students submit stories to writing contests every year but never to a bonafide publisher. The thought of showing my book to a professional of any kind in the writing business terrified me. It had been a long time since I had dazzled the editor of the community newspaper.

I went to the fridge, took out some milk and poured myself a huge bowl of cereal. I went back to the wobbly card table and placed the bowl next to the keyboard. When I sat down, my stomach banged into the table and milk sloshed over the rim of the cereal bowl. I looked down at the milk. It reminded me of Mrs. Peach's white leather jacket. She must be very happy that I was gone. I pulled off my shirt and used it to wipe up the spilled milk. Then I opened up the online news and scrolled through the headlines while I ate my cereal. There were several headlines about the province-wide job action that the teachers' union had just launched and about Bill 1010. I didn't open any of the articles. I was glad to be out of it. I thought about my final day in the classroom, just myself and the kids, telling stories, connecting. There was space to breathe. Space to express. Space. Freedom. I imagined what it would have been like for Olga in Mexico. She had spent a full year teaching without school supplies, just an empty classroom, just herself and the kids, their voices, their imaginations, their bodies. No wonder she was so beautifully intimidating—the woman was not afraid to be free.

There was a knock on the basement door. I put my shirt back on, which was still wet from the spilled milk.

It was James. Dressed in black as usual, but with an unusually bright expression on his face. I hadn't heard from him since I'd left him behind in Positano, and I could tell something was up.

"Look at you down here in your man cave," said James, grinning. He patted me heartily on the wettest part of my shirt as he followed me inside. "Is that sweat?" he said, making a face as he looked at his damp hand. "Tell me it's not."

"It's not."

"I'm not going to ask!"

I could sense his enthusiasm. He was vigorous and animated.

"When did you get back?" I asked. "Do you want a drink? Milk? Beer?"

"Yesterday," said James, "and no thanks…" He hesitated before adding, "Philomena is waiting for me in the car. I just stopped by to ask you something."

I faced him, studying his expression to see if this was a joke. "You didn't bring her back with you. Did you?"

"We're getting married," he said, thrusting his hand out so that I could shake it, "and we owe it all to you and your trip to Hades. Thanks, Beast."

I took James's hand and let him pump it up and down several times.

"Married? When?"

"In four weeks—first weekend in May," he said, letting go of my hand. "I want you to be my best man, and we'll invite Olga, too. Women love weddings. Maybe it'll help you get her out of the dreaded friend-zone."

"Maybe. If she does actually want to be more than friends with me."

"Don't get so hung up on that. She likes you. I don't know why. But she does—so are you going to be my best man or what?"

"Best man? She's really here? You're really getting married?"

"Please don't make me beg."

"Her parents are okay with this?"

"Yes."

"Well…then…yes!…of course."

I was still in a kind of unbelieving stupor when James slapped me hard on the shoulder and turned to go.

At the door he said, "Great. I want a stag party. Next weekend. Friday night."

"Right," I muttered, "Friday night."

"Next Friday."

"Right."

"One week from today."

"Right."

"And good luck on your date with Olga. Let me—let *us* know how it goes."

After he left, I finally had the nerve to call Olga and set up our date.

There was no answer.

5

It was Saturday evening, date night. My first date since 1986. And I wasn't worried at all.

Right.

With plenty of time, I thought, to make our eight o'clock, two-hundred-dollar, special "Carlo" reservation, I pulled up in front of a surprisingly ordinary, beige apartment building that was just a few blocks up from beach in Kitsilano. The windows were small and rimmed with water stains and cracked stucco; there were no verandas or flowering window boxes, just a few stumpy evergreen shrubs pressed up against the beige walls of the ground floor. It was not the kind of place I imagined Olga living in; it was so plain, so un-extraordinary, until Olga appeared in the lobby in a black, off-the-shoulder dress with a red wrap and black high heels, and the mundane setting suddenly became palatial, and it was hard to breathe. She smiled at me as she let herself out of the building into the still-sunny evening. Then she was walking down the sidewalk towards me, with her hair pulled back in a low bun which highlighted her smile, in that black dress which highlighted her curves; and I didn't dare get out of the car. I couldn't. Trying to calm myself down, I lifted my hand off the steering wheel and waved at her. She smiled even more brightly at me and waved back. Then she was at the passenger-side door; and I was still sitting there, like an idiot, staring at her, calming myself down, trying to think of something charming to say when she got in.

But she didn't get in; she was waiting for something.

My intestinal fortitude went soft. Something was wrong: she had sized up me, and my car with the fist-shaped dent in the hood, and had changed her mind about the date. That was it. She wanted to be friends, nothing more. I had already blown it, and I hadn't even said hello yet. Then I clued in.

I swung open the door and got out quickly. "I'm sorry!" I said as I hurried around the front of the car and opened the passenger door for her.

"Thank you, Harry," she said. Then, without hesitation, she bent down to sweep stale muffin crumbs off the passenger seat.

I stood there on the sidewalk, dumbly staring, until her hips stopped wiggling, and she got in the car.

"You look really nice," I said at the exact moment I closed the door.

Olga looked at me quizzically through the windshield as I walked around the car.

I got in beside her.

She looked at me, smiling. "I'm sorry. I didn't hear what you said."

"Sorry about the crumbs and...," I adjusted myself in the seat and turned the key in the ignition, even though the car was already running, "—oops, sorry about the noise—I said you look really nice."

"Thank you, Harry. You look really nice too."

I glanced at her and added, "I thought about showing up naked...you know...for our naked date, so...yeah...I probably look better like this than I would like that... I would have scared you off—big hairy naked guys are terrifying..."

Olga laughed out loud; it sounded like bells, the bells from the cathedral by the sea in Positano, with a hallelujah Vatican chorus on the side. It was a tender, sweet, innocent-but-knowing laugh that disarmed me completely and took me back to the view from my veranda on the cliffside. I was a puddle of sap.

I, who never got lost, took two wrong turns, which made us late for our dinner reservation.

We arrived at Carlo's cousin's restaurant twenty minutes past my two-hundred-dollar reservation time. Believing that we might not get a table at all, I hustled Olga, unceremoniously, out of the car, forgetting the souvenirs from Positano that were in the back, and hurried her up to the restaurant entryway. I had gone on at length during the drive about how this was my contractor's cousin's place, how it was a true taste of Italy, which became even more exciting when I found out that Italy was one of the few countries Olga had not visited. So when I swept open the door for her and saw that the restaurant was half-empty, not crammed with customers waving money at the hostess to get them a table, I was mad.

"What is it?" Olga asked as she sat down in the chair that was being held out for her by the waiter.

"It's just not what I expected," I said as I scanned the restaurant for someone who might be Carlo's cousin. I wanted a refund.

"You mean it's not like Italy?"

"Sort of." That reminded me of the souvenirs. "I'll be right back. I brought you some things from Positano." I stood up and started to leave.

Olga grabbed the edge of my sports jacket and said, playfully, "It can wait, Harry. Sit down, and let's have a drink. I want to hear about Italy and your book."

I'm not sure it was possible to love her more than I already did, but in three simple sentences and tug on the hem of my sports jacket, I fell even deeper for her. Of course, I sat myself back down immediately.

"What kind of wine do you like?" I asked, opening the menu.

Just then, Olga's cell phone rang.

"I'm sorry," she said. "I forgot to turn it off. How rude of me."

I closed the menu and stood up. Olga looked up at me. She didn't look pleased.

"You know what? Take the call. I'm going out to the car to get your gift."

She nodded and took the call.

When I came back with the lemon-dotted apron and five bars of lemon-shaped soap, Olga looked even more displeased. I put the gifts on the table and asked tentatively, "Are you okay?"

Olga reached across the table and stopped just short of touching the back of my hand. Her smile was subdued. I called the waiter over and, in nervous Italian, ordered a bottle of Neapolitan red and seafood appetizers. Olga smiled and seemed truly impressed by my fumbling linguistic abilities.

She asked, "How is your book coming along?"

I watched the waiter uncork and pour the wine.

"I haven't written a word since I've been back. I've been busy with the house and, honestly, I'm running out of steam."

"Are you running out of ideas?"

"No, it's not that. It's more that I don't know what I'm going to do with it when it's done."

"Let me read it," Olga offered.

The thought of her reading it terrified me. What if she thought I was an imbecile? I shrugged. "Maybe...sure...when it's finished."

"I respect your courage." Olga rotated her wine glass slowly by the stem. "Did you put some of your personal stories in it, like the one you told your students?"

I shook my head. "So far it's been like writing a dissertation. It seemed like the best way to approach it—seriously, like a big essay. I want to change the way we do education in North America, the way we do everything here these days. I really hate how dependent we are on computers and video games. You know...well, I know you know. You're the naked storyteller. That's why I like you so much. I love how you taught your students in Mexico."

A tremor ran across her delicate features. I wanted to come over and kiss her, then kneel down and ask her to marry me. But I didn't. I had more wine and waited for her to continue.

"I miss it, Harry. I'd like to go back. I loved my naked classroom, with just the students and I learning from each other. Truthfully, if you had shown up tonight nude and riding a horse to take me to a wiener roast at Wreck Beach, I would have been okay with that. All this—," she gestured at herself as if to mean her make up and her outfit, the tablecloth, the restaurant, Hastings Street, and Vancouver itself, "—it's complicating."

Not even when I was a teenager had I ever wanted to kiss a woman so badly.

"My classroom wasn't empty for much more than an hour," I said, "but it was an amazing hour."

Olga lifted her glass by the stem and took a gentle sip. "Do you think you could do what I did? Run away to Mexico to teach children who have nothing, with nothing other than your voice, your body and your stories?"

"Yes."

She looked directly at me. "You could put that in your book."

"I could."

Olga smiled. She seemed relaxed and unguarded again.

"Were you able to teach your students in Mexico to read and write?"

She nodded and smiled. "As much as I could. We didn't have any supplies for the first year I was there—no pencils or pens or books or paper of any kind, until a foreign journalist wrote an article about us. Then we were inundated with school supplies from sponsors in the States, but before then, it was all stories and…," she laughed, "I had them drawing in the mud with sticks on days after it rained, which weren't many."

"Wow. Sticks and mud…"

I leaned back so the waiter could put out the appetizer plates and put the food down between us. "It's hard to imagine. Do you know how they're doing now?"

"There is a proper school there now, with six teachers and laptops that run on solar power. I'm not sure how much storytelling takes place any more. I'd like to go back and see if the students remember the stories we made up together that first year."

"We definitely need more of that here—storytelling, I mean. As far as the union and the administration are concerned, I really screwed up, but I think," I leaned over my plate, "some of the kids were really engaged by my story, and they all seemed to appreciate being given the opportunity to tell their own stories. They thought it was weird at first, but they got into it. I mean really got into it."

"I think you should put your story in your book."

"The one I told my kids?"

"It's funny. You should, leopard-print panties and all," she winked.

That caught me off guard. I hadn't told her the part about Cindy. Who had? Cautiously, I said, "I hadn't planned on it. I'm trying to sound credible. There is a lot of bias against storytelling. Most educators say that past kindergarten, it has no place in the formal education system. One Dr. So-and-so says storytelling is all lies and has no place in education, not even in kindergarten."

Olga shook her head. "They have no idea. Good for you, Harry. I think your book will be—"

"—a best seller?"

"I hope so," she said, putting her hand on mine. "You deserve it."

"Thank you," I said, wanting to turn my hand over and lace my fingers through hers. I wanted to, but I was afraid that if I twitched, the moment would be over.

She slid her hand away, back to the stem of her wine glass. Before I could say anything, she looked at me and smiled warmly.

"Thanks for taking me out tonight, Harry. I'm having fun. You're more than I expected."

I tore off a piece of bread and dipped it in a dish of olive oil and balsamic vinegar. I chewed slowly as I watched Olga slice a scallop into two perfectly even pieces.

After I swallowed, I said, "I need to apologize for something."

Olga looked up from her plate. "I can't imagine what for," she said quietly.

"The first email I sent you from Positano, I didn't mean to tell you...everything. I am sorry for putting you on the spot like that. I mean you're gorgeous and smart, and I think any man would be lucky to even see you walk down the street. I didn't think you could possibly feel the same way about me. We hadn't even gone out yet. That was stupid of me. It was the wine and sitting out on that balcony overlooking the Mediterranean. It touched me, the wine and that view..."

Olga looked alarmed and hurt. She spoke, her voice tight. "It was just the wine and the view that made you write that beautiful letter?"

"No! No!" I said, angry with myself for putting her on the spot again. "I mean, I felt it. I feel it. But I had no right to tell you so soon. I just wanted to tell you, so I did. I'm sorry, and now I'm sorry for making tonight awkward."

Olga relaxed and smiled. "I'm glad you meant it. Now...I have to tell you something."

My guts tightened.

"Harry, I'm here with you tonight even though..."

Her smile was completely gone.

My stomach gurgled loudly, and I knew I was about to pass some wicked gas, so I had to excuse myself—urgently—regardless of Olga's reaction to my sudden departure from the table.

As I sat on the toilet, I debated whether or not I wanted to know the end of that sentence: "I'm here with you even though..." Was she seeing someone else? That would explain her comment about getting to know me as a friend. Should I ask her about that or just let it go and focus on getting her to say yes to a second date? I pondered my next move as I washed my hands.

As soon as I sat down, the waiter slid over to our table. He took our dinner orders and refilled our glasses. As soon as he slid away, Olga sighed.

Not wanting to get into anything heavy, I blurted out, "James is getting married."

Olga gave me a half smile, a knowing smile. I could tell she was willing to play along with me and keep it light, at least for the moment.

I barged on as delicately as I could. "He met a girl in Positano, and she flew back with him. I'm supposed to throw a bachelor party next Friday."

"I had coffee with Philomena today. She is a lovely girl."

"You did?"

"James called me earlier in the week and asked me to show her around town and help her get settled. I didn't mind. She's a nice girl, and brave," Olga nodded her head slowly, "very brave. James is the one who told me about the leopard-print panties and the pizza. You poor man."

"I see. Some friend he is." Picking up my wine glass, I said, "Would you do that, move to a new country with someone you just met?"

"Maybe I already have." Olga sat back in her chair, holding her wine glass in front of her. "You haven't asked me if I've ever been married or have children."

It was true. It hadn't even crossed my mind. I had been so focused on not screwing things up, I hadn't asked any of the hard questions that people on first dates usually ask each other.

She leaned forward, rested her elbows on the table, and looked right into my eyes.

After a moment, she said, "Aren't you just a little bit curious?"

I did my best to return the eye contact, but my eyes kept drifting to the inch of cleavage that was showing in the dip of her dress.

"Have you? Do you?" I asked.

"Married once, but no children, for ten years. And I should be honest with you, that was him on the phone. He's just turned fifty, and he's having second thoughts."

I chuckled to mask my panic and said jokingly, "Trust me, no man gets to have second thoughts about turning fifty. And if he does, too bad. Fifty hits hard; there is nothing you can do about it." I chuckled again.

Olga looked at me like she was my mom, and I was an eight-year-old who had just lied to her about brushing my teeth. "You know what I meant. My ex-husband is having second thoughts about us...as a couple. He says he wants me back. Ever since I got back from my tour, he hasn't left me alone."

"I see."

I really didn't see. I just wanted to know the guy's name and address so that my sledgehammer and I could drop by later.

"Rally is upset that I came out with you tonight. I wouldn't be surprised if he showed up here. He was the one who brought me to this restaurant once, when we were first dating."

I glanced at the door. I could feel my pores open and sweat start to eek out. "You told him where we are?"

Olga nodded and took a sip of water. "I'm sorry. Rally has this ability to catch me off guard and make me feel like I'm doing something wrong. He always wants to know where I am and who I'm with. He's controlling. That's why I left him. I want to be able to live...be myself." She looked at me hopefully. "I want to be loved unconditionally, Harry—unconditionally. Do you understand?"

I nodded and should have said something like: "I wouldn't care what you did or who you were with," or "I love you just the way you are," or "you're perfect," but I was worried, again, about coming on too strong, while another part of my brain was wondering just how controlling this guy, Rally, was, and what I would do if he showed up, and why the name sounded familiar.

"What does he do?"

"He's a reporter," she said. "Rally Kite. You two might have been colleagues if you had stayed with the newspaper. I don't think you would have been friends, though." She shook her head and added, "But I don't want to talk about him. I want to talk about you, Harry. Tell me a story, a fun story from Italy."

Over a dinner that was a fairly good attempt at authentic Italian cuisine, though not worth the extra two hundred, I told Olga stories about driving the Amalfi Coast, the erotic art in Pompeii and the view from my apartment in Positano. It was after midnight when we left the restaurant and walked to the car, side by side, so close to each other we were almost touching. The night was clear, but the spring breeze still carried a chill. We decided after a few wobbly steps down the sidewalk that we needed to find a Jitters before I did any driving, but after walking up and down both sides of the near-deserted street, we gave up looking for lattes and sat down at a bus stop. Olga opened her red wrap and used it like a blanket around her shoulders. She shivered slightly.

"Can I put my arm around you?" I asked at the same moment that my arm, of its own volition, wrapped itself tightly around her shoulders and hugged her close.

"What if I said no?" said Olga, putting her head on my shoulder.

"I'd do it anyway," I said.

We sat quietly together for a few moments, until I impatiently broke the silence.

"Can I kiss you?"

Olga lifted her head and looked up at me, and then stood up.

I knew then, I had crossed a line and had ruined everything. I was about to stand up too, when Olga turned and sat down on my lap, wrapped her arms around my neck and shoulders and kissed me hard on the lips. I sucked in my gut, pulled her even closer and kissed her back. When we surfaced a while later, I knew it was time to drive her home. I needed to come up with an idea for a second date, fast.

"What are you thinking?" she whispered in my ear.

I had never been to Wreck Beach, but at that particular moment I was thinking about what it would be like to lie in the warm sand next to her. "Do you want to come over and see my reno tomorrow afternoon?" As soon as I said it, I regretted it.

"I'd love to, but I'm telling a story at a pet funeral tomorrow afternoon."

I was too surprised by the creativity of her excuse to press for details, and I had no other idea for a second date, except Wreck Beach, but it was still April and cool.

I said hurriedly, "Okay. I'd better get you home."

Wallowing up to my beard in disappointment and rejection, I lifted Olga off my lap, got up and started walking away from the bus stop.

Olga stood there, not following. Then she called after me.

I stopped and turned around. I was crushed by the realization this would be our only date.

"Aren't you going to hold my hand?" she said, sweetly, tenderly, without a trace of disinterest.

I came back to her, cursing myself for being so tentative. I reached down and picked her up.

"Harry! You're going to drop me! I'm too heavy," she laughed.

"You're perfect, a feather."

She nestled her head on my shoulder and was silent until we were almost at the car.

She whispered, "You're not planning to turn this into a naked date, are you?"

I kissed her, then I carried her—without too much effort thanks to all the stairs in Positano—the rest of the way to the car, helped her inside and drove her to her apartment, where I kissed her goodnight and floated all the way home.

6

"This is crazy, Harry," laughed Olga as she brushed past the *Clothing Optional* sign at the top of the Wreck Beach trail. "It's probably going to rain on us." She started down the steep steps ahead of me.

I was enjoying the tangy scent of the cedar forest with its tall, cliffside trees that formed a deep green canopy overhead. I was also enjoying the movement of Olga's hips wiggling in her black yoga pants as she descended, keeping at least five steps ahead of me.

"Then we'll have the place to ourselves," I said.

"Are you planning on going nude when we get down there?"

I held up the picnic blanket I was carrying. "Down to my toga at least."

She laughed. "These steps aren't going to be fun on the way up."

"After Positano, this is nothing," I bragged. "I'll carry you up if you get tired."

Olga looked over her shoulder and gave me a stunning smile. I was so affected by it that I missed a step, almost dropped our muffins, coffee and my blanket-toga, and had to grab the log railing to stay on my feet.

"Are you falling for me, Harry Tyke?" Olga teased as she took the coffee out of my hands.

I nodded and gave her a goofy grin, which confirmed I was.

When we reached the bottom and stepped out onto the sand, she said, "This is prettier than I imagined."

Straight ahead, the beach jutted out and became a breakwater where the river met the sea. To our right, the swath of sand curved and wrapped itself around the base of the treed cliffs before disappearing around the point. Long, driftwood logs lined the swath of sand in staggered rows. Balancing the coffee tray in one hand, Olga reached down and took off her running shoes and socks. The sand was grey and smooth, but filled with bits of driftwood and small sticks. I followed her lead, but immediately regretted it; the beach debris was sharp on my tender feet.

She looked up and down the deserted beach. "Where should we go?"

"I have no idea. How about we follow the cliff around to the point? The tide is low enough that we can get around, I think."

I offered her my free hand. She took it with hers.

"When do I get to see you in your toga?" she asked.

"I think I had better keep the blanket handy just in case some young stallion pops up from behind a log, and I need to cover your eyes."

Olga started laughing so hard that she stopped walking. "Oh, Harry. Stop. I'm old. You can't make me laugh like that, not without a bathroom close by."

I pulled her close and kissed her. She fell heavily into me. I pulled her even closer. "What time is your pet funeral?" I delicately asked.

"Two o'clock."

"The sun is trying to come out. I think we should have our breakfast."

Olga smiled and nodded, so I led her to a rectangle of sand that was bordered on three sides by large logs and on one side by the steep cliff. I lay the blanket down and pulled her gently down onto it.

"You know, Harry, when I think of things like a naked classroom or a naked date, I don't mean nude. I mean: no noise, no stuff, no wine, no fancy dress or hair in a bun, no car, no restaurant. I mean you and I, just the two of us, our minds and our bodies and our hearts. That's what I mean when I say naked."

I propped my head up on my elbow and wrapped my other arm around the dip in her waist. "I love your idea of naked, but I would really like to introduce you to mine."

Olga laughed. She reached over and stroked my beard. "I'm sure you would, old guy. I'm sure you would."

A while later, we sat side by side on a log quietly eating our muffins and sipping our coffees, looking out at the waves and distant, curvaceous string of islands. Olga had the sandy blanket wrapped around her shoulders. I used a corner of it to wipe the sweat off my face.

Without looking away from the water, she asked, "So what are your plans for the future?"

I had to swallow a big piece of bran muffin before I could answer.

Once I rinsed my mouth out with coffee, I said, "I was thinking about giving a writing career a try. Finish my book. And I'd like to go back to Italy."

"No more teaching?"

I held back the part about my refusal to do twenty sessions with the union-appointed psychologist. "Not the way things are going. I'm the old guy who thinks kids should address adults by their last name and walk to school and play outside. I drive around with a sledgehammer in the trunk of my car, a real Luddite."

She laughed at me. "That must feel good."

I smiled. "Not as good as being with you."

"So the old guy is rebooting his life?" she teased.

"Not reboot. How about retell?"

Olga leaned against me. "I love that, Harry." Cautiously, it seemed, she pressed further. "How are you going to finance this literary adventure if you quit teaching?"

"After the renos, I'm selling my house. It's a two-million-dollar anchor around my neck. And, besides," I ventured, "I don't need such a big place," I hugged her tightly, "even if—"

"—if what?" she said, springing upright. She turned and looked up at me, "—if I move in with you?"

I grinned and shrugged.

She shook her head at me, and I once again felt like a scolded child, not a neglected one, but one who is lovingly chastised for his own betterment.

"Harry Tyke, you are getting so far ahead of yourself that you are tripping over your own rear end!"

I laughed and put my arm around her, reeling her back in. She settled into my chest and looked out at the water.

"What about your students?" she asked after a moment. "You could keep trying to bring stories into the classroom."

I looked down at the top of her head and said, "I'm going to get rid of that house. It owes me. It owes me a life."

Olga sighed.

"What's wrong?"

"I don't want to go, but I need to get ready for my gig and… my lunch date."

"Lunch date?"

"I'm meeting Rally."

I instantly stiffened and removed my arm from the curvy dip in her waist.

"Sorry. Not a date, wrong choice of words. I'm meeting Rally for lunch before my gig. I'm going to make it clear that we are finished. I'm not going back. He doesn't get a second chance."

I slipped my arm back around her waist and kissed her. Then we pulled apart, and I looked down at her dark eyes and mildly red face.

"You scared me."

"I have no intention of going backwards, Harry. I'm getting too old for that. There is a lot I still want to do, and I'm not willing to let anyone stand in my way. Your house is an anchor; Rally was my anchor. I'd never go back to that again." She was thoughtful for a moment, then added, "It's the wrong way to live."

I was all sap, and I gushed, "You are an amazing and beautiful woman, Olga. I have never met anyone like you. I never imagined a woman like you existed. I know you said you just wanted to be friends, but I am in love with you."

Olga laughed and patted my chest, and said, "Let's go, old guy. You need to hit those stairs and get that body of yours in shape so that you can keep up with me."

She bent over and started putting her shoes back on. She finished lacing up first and then took off like a shot along a log.

"Race you to the top!" she called.

I watched her slim figure balance and jump from log to log. My legs were still weak and twitching, but being around Olga gave me a buoyancy I had not experienced since my youth. As soon as I finished tying up my laces, I used my longer legs to catch up. I passed her before we reached the bottom of the stairs and somehow, with the blanket draped over my shoulders like a legionnaire's cape, managed to beat her to the top flight of stairs.

She was hardly winded as we stepped together onto the landing at the top of the cliff. I tried to match her relaxed breathing pattern, but my heart was trying to beat its way out of the top of my skull, and my heaving lungs would not stop shuddering.

"Just give me a second," I said as I bent double and heaved for oxygen.

Olga took the blanket off my shoulders and draped it over her own. "Don't have a heart attack."

"I'm not," I heaved defensively. "I won't."

"No, you can't."

I stood up and said, "Race you to the car."

Olga shook her head and grabbed my hand before I could take off. She put my arm around her shoulders and let me lean on her as we walked to the car.

That evening, exhausted from the morning's exercise, I sat at my wobbly card table, vibrating with anticipation because Olga was coming over in less than an hour. We had just finished a lengthy phone conversation, during which she had explained that she had been paid four hundred dollars to do a professional telling of the birth and adoption story of a family's beloved pure-bred St. Bernard, named Oliver, that had tragically succumbed to cancer during middle age. That had quickly turned into a discussion of childhood pets, in which Olga mentioned that she was allergic to all furry creatures, and that the only pet she had ever had was Rally's cat, which had given her hives every day of their marriage. I had asked Olga if she might be allergic to me. She suggested, as a joke, that I give up my beard. There had been an awkward silence for a moment while I considered going hairless; but then Olga started asking me about my book and got on me to put my own stories in the final chapters. I didn't feel it was the right approach, but she sold me on the idea that showing is better than telling, and that I should seriously think about adding a personal story to the book. Then we made plans to go out for the evening. Olga had asked if she could come over and see the renovations before we went out. At first, I had said no, because I didn't want her to see my mess, but somehow, by the end of the phone call, she had me saying yes.

I got up and studied my bachelor pad: the food wrappers and empty bottles on the bar, the unmade sofa bed and pile of laundry. Perhaps I had made a mistake inviting her over and could minimize the damage by whisking her out the door after a brief tour of the main floor.

I was in the shower when the phone rang. Normally, I wouldn't have bothered to answer, but I thought it might be Olga needing directions. It wasn't. It was the director of Canterbury Care Home. My mother had had a stroke and was being transported to the hospital. I listened. I nodded, dutifully though artificially. Then I hung up and stood dripping on the thinning carpet, debating whether or not I should cancel my date with Olga. As I towelled off, something like guilt got me by the shorthairs, and I went to the hospital to see Adelle Tyke.

7

"What's wrong with you?" Adelle slurred.

What's wrong, I answered silently, is that I'm here with you instead of with someone who actually likes me. Adelle had become increasingly agitated during my visit. By that point, I had been keeping my cool for over two hours; the insults were starting to sting.

"Why can't you just leave my house the way it was, you stupid boy?" she said, her tone snappy and rude.

The stroke had aggravated her already angry demeanour but, from my point of view, not by much. She startled me when she tried to slap my cheek. I pulled back in time, so she barely grazed my beard.

"Harold, why won't you shave that thing off?"

I rubbed my beard thoughtfully. "Because."

"You could never look after things properly. Driving around in that horrid car. Never satisfied with anything we did for you. It's my house. It's my house! It's perfect the way it is. No one gave you the right—you can't touch it! You don't have the right."

"Actually, I do have the right."

The nurse came in just then, so I said sweetly, "Just rest, Mom." I patted her translucent, blue-grey hand. "We'll talk about the house tomorrow."

"You need to keep her calm, please," said the nurse, looking at me over her glasses as she gave Adelle an injection. "Why don't you go get your mom some flowers, something to brighten up the room."

Adelle grimaced at me for a few seconds, then her eyes went glassy and the lids closed. I sank deeper into the vinyl chair beside her bed and steeled myself for a very long, very uncomfortable night. I smiled weakly at the nurse when she left, promising not to upset "Mom." Then we were alone, mother and son, Adelle and Harold, contentiously coexisting, just like the old days.

Adelle was thin, grey and square, thinner, greyer and squarer than I had ever seen her. Stripped of make up, her complexion was paler than the pillow case. Her eyes were mostly closed, but, from time to time, they would roll open, and she would grimace at me. When she made her faces, I smiled insincerely, patted her hand and said things like: "Your house is fine. Just as nice as it always was. I was just kidding. I would never change a thing. I would never sell it. It's perfect. I'll live there forever in my old bedroom. And your cuckoo clock is fixed, runs better than ever." The edges of her mouth would turn upwards in a faint smile, and she would doze off again. I wanted to go home. I could have gone home. But I sat there, wondering when she would die so that I could put in her the family plot next to Ken, and she could rest assured that he was hers forever, that over all the other young women my father had chased, and who had chased him, she was now the only one; he finally belonged completely to her.

I woke up the next morning when Adelle smacked me on the forehead with a rolled up magazine. "Get up, lazy creature," she slurred. "I'm dying. I want grapefruit juice. Fresh squeezed!"

I went across the street to the nearest Jitters and bought my mother the only grapefruit juice they had, which was not fresh squeezed, and myself an extra-large coffee. I was maneuvering the tray so that I could open the door, when Otto Logan appeared and swung it open for me so abruptly I lost my balance and almost fell on the sidewalk.

"Mr. Tyke!" he exclaimed, his thin face bright, eyes wide. "We thought you were dead."

"Otto! No," said his mother, shaking her head at him. "I'm sorry, Mr. Tyke. It's nice to see you again."

"Shouldn't you be at school?" I asked.

His mother smiled. "We had an early appointment with the psychiatrist today. Otto keeps telling a certain story over and over again." She winked. "We love his enthusiasm but..."

"I'm so sorry about that." I did feel bad for Otto's parents. "You must be glad to have a new teacher."

"No, Mr. Tyke! We miss you. You should see. We all got our new laptops after spring break, and everyone wants you to show us how to write stories like you do. Now that you're alive again, can you come back to class? Can you?"

Otto's mom was mouthing the word yes and nodding her head so that I would tell Otto what he wanted to hear. I promised him I would be back soon.

"How about today? My mom is taking me to school, right after she buys me a barely warm hot chocolate with no whipping cream and only half the chocolate. We can drive you. Right, Mom?"

"Mr. Tyke looks like he has somewhere to be."

I nodded. "That's right. My mother is in the hospital."

"Can we go to the hospital with Mr. Tyke and see his mom? I would really like to see her shoulder pads."

I knew that under his raincoat, Otto was very likely wearing an orange t-shirt with homemade shoulder pads.

"Okay, Otto," said Mrs. Logan, putting her hands on her son's shoulders and steering him inside. "Say goodbye to Mr. Tyke."

"Mom! I want to see her shoulder pads."

He was winding up for a flail. I could see it.

"Nice to see you, Otto," I said.

"Mr. Tyke," said Mrs. Logan, pausing, "Greg is a part-time comedian, and he told me the other night that you should come and tell your story at The Cave. They have an amateur hour every other Friday before the main acts. He thinks you'd be great."

"Thanks," was all I managed to say. The compliment surprised me.

"Got to run now, before Otto starts telling your story to everyone inside. Here's my husband's card."

I took the card and watched her pulled her flailing son towards the counter.

Back in Adelle's room, I put the juice down on the breakfast tray. Seeing the bed empty, the waiting nurse and the bathroom door closed, I guessed my mother was up.

The toilet flushed.

I spoke quickly and quietly to the nurse. "Can you tell her I brought the grapefruit juice, and that I have to get to work?"

"Liar!" shouted Adelle as she tried to push open the heavy door. "Walter Magee's mother told me you lost your job!"

Walter Magee was a pharmacist with two kids at Dugwood.

"I'm on leave," I corrected her.

"Liar!" she shouted.

"Hush, Mrs. Tyke," said the nurse. "I think you should go," she said to me, keeping her voice low. "Your mother is extremely agitated." She guided Adelle into the waiting wheelchair.

"Liar! Thief!" Adelle shrieked at me as she folded her papery figure in the wheelchair and let the nurse wheel her over to the bed.

To the nurse she lowered her voice and said with conviction, "I asked my son to bring me fresh apple juice, and he brings me this rat poison. He wants to change my house—my house! He thinks I'm a stupid old woman. But I can see what he's trying to do. I'm not stupid."

"Mrs. Tyke," said the nurse, trying to get my mother back in bed without knocking over the breakfast tray, "you must calm down."

I walked out of the room, wishing, not for the first time, that I had a sibling who could help me deal with her, but I wouldn't have wished Adelle Tyke on anyone.

When I pulled up in front of my house—my house—it was after ten, and I didn't see Carlo's truck parked on the street. Annoyed, I grabbed the mail and went inside. I put my phone on speaker and dialled Carlo's number. As it rang, I sifted through the mail. There was the usual newsletter from the Alliance of Teachers and an invitation to James and Philomena's wedding.

"*Salve*, Teacher," said Carlo.

"It's Monday morning. Why aren't you putting that wall back in today? Where is your crew?"

"My framer is on another job this week. Next Monday, we do your wall."

"Can't you get started on something else: the kitchen or the bathroom? What about the fireplace?"

"No possible. We do wall first."

I considered blasting Carlo for conning me out of two hundred dollars for that useless dinner reservation, but I didn't want to get on his bad side and have to find another contractor. Like Olga, I wanted to go forward, not backward. So I said, "Fine. Next Monday, then."

"*Si*, next Monday." Carlo hung up without saying *ciao* or asking about my date.

With the renovations now stalled for a week, I was at a loss. I supposed I should get back to my book. With a some effort and minimal distractions, I could probably knock off the last few chapters fairly quickly. I also supposed I should start arranging James's stag party or call Otto's dad to find out about amateur night. I could also get a haircut, trim my beard, buy some new clothes, go for a run, get a gym membership, or even go back to the hospital and visit my lovely mother. Instead of doing any of those productive, purposeful things, I browsed real estate websites looking at properties in Positano and researching listings in my neighbourhood, until Olga called and invited me over for dinner.

We had a beautiful evening. Her cooking was delicious, and her apartment felt like home. She modelled the apron with lemons on it that I had bought for her in Positano. We drank a very expensive bottle of wine that I had splurged on after buying the biggest bouquet of flowers I could find at the florist's. We talked about the places we had travelled to and the places we still wanted to see. We talked about the ending for my book, the teachers' job action and Bill 1010. We talked about whether or not a foot massage and sweet nothings were enough to get a woman into bed and whether or not lawyers and psychologists are worth their astronomical rates. What we didn't talk about was Rally's sudden interest in Olga or Adelle's stroke, but we did brainstorm ideas for James's bachelor party, none of which she approved of.

There were moments during the evening when Olga was as youthful and adventurous as a teenager and others when she seemed more like she was trying to be my mother. I had never met a woman who was such a mixture of ages. When she changed gears it threw me, but, somehow, I never felt ill at ease around her. It had only been three dates, but I didn't want to go home that night; I wanted to spend every moment of the coming week with her. But it didn't work out that way.

8

It was Friday night, and I had my hatchback barreling full-tilt down the I-5 freeway towards a casino and resort partway between Bellingham and Seattle. I wasn't feeling the party spirit. The night before, I had eaten an entire bag of pizza-flavoured nut mix while watching the original Conan movie. The nuts had given me terrible heartburn, which kept me awake all night. All day, I felt like I had a rock in my esophagus; a hard bubble of gas was wedged in my chest like a fist.

James was in the passenger seat. James's father, Norm, a semi-retired accountant, two years my senior, who absolutely loved his job and surfing, sat in the backseat with James's childhood friend, Pierre. I had bought tickets for a comedy show at the casino, but the three-hour border line up had us running really late. On top of the fist in my esophagus, I wasn't in the mood for a night out. I hadn't seen Olga once since our third date. She had been putting me off all week, rejecting all of my romantic date ideas, saying she was too busy helping Philomena get ready for the wedding during the day and teaching a series of storytelling workshops in the evenings. I tried to believe her, but I was still haunted by her "just friends" statement. She had, after all, put it in writing. The spectre of Rally Kite was there as well, in the gloom of my mood. The worry had stopped me from writing, from doing anything other than moping around the basement, eating too much, thinking too much, and doing far too little, especially for a man who was trying to reclaim his life.

I gripped the steering wheel as a wave of pressure spasmed in my chest. A tiny squeak of air escaped through my mouth, but it wasn't enough to relieve the discomfort. I had a terrible urge to turn around and go back to my man cave, but I suppressed it.

James, who had been talking with his father about possible venues for the wedding reception, looked at me and asked, "So are we going to make it?"

"To the show? Not likely."

Pierre leaned forward and asked, "How many rooms did you book?"

"One," I said.

Norm asked, "You mean a suite with two rooms and four beds, right, buddy?"

I shook my head.

"Don't worry, Dad," said James. "We'll get another room when we get there."

"So, Harry," said Norm, being overly friendly, "James says you're writing a book."

I was not in the mood for small talk. "I'm trying," I said, glancing at Norm's smug, handsome, surfer face in the cracked rearview mirror.

He said, with a knowing smirk and a twinkle, "I've written six books on surfing. I tell you, the publishing business is a dog-eat-dog world, even when you have connections. When you're starting out at the bottom, it's tough. I'm glad I wasn't foolish enough to try to make a living at it. With ten percent royalties on books that sell for about ten dollars, you don't take enough home to worry about. I can't imagine how writers make a living. Accounting has been good to me, really good. Right, Son?" he said, putting his hand on James's shoulder. "We've had a pretty good life. Mostly because of your beautiful mother."

"Sure, Dad. We've had a great life. But you and Mom never spoiled me. Harry says kids today are so spoiled it's making them stupid because they never have to do anything for themselves."

"Wow! Do you really think that, Harry?" asked Pierre.

Norm laughed. "Harry'll like this, then. James's mother and I wanted him to work for everything. Son, we were tickled when you told us you were going into teaching. I swear, Harry, the kid has been playing teacher since he was in preschool. Remember the Christmas when you wanted us to redo your room like the inside of a classroom? What a project that was, but you were so excited. You brought the neighbourhood kids over every day to play school. Right, Pierre? You were always there."

"I sure was," echoed Pierre, right on cue.

I wanted to stop the car and kick them all out.

Norm continued reminiscing. "Then there was the day you told us you had enough of a down payment for your condo and enough income from teaching that you didn't need us to co-sign your mortgage. That was another good day for us."

I rolled my eyes. Norm leaned forward again to talk to me. I hated that he was right behind me, gripping the sides of my seat, breathing on me.

"Like I was saying, Harry. I've had six books published on surfing but haven't made enough on them to buy this car. You're not planning to make a living as a writer, are you?"

"I'm thinking about it."

Pierre spoke up. "That's brave at your age."

"Is it?" I asked.

"Leave him alone, Pierre. I'm sure the man's been investing in the market all these years? What about your wife, Harry, does she bring in a decent salary?"

"I'm divorced, and I'm not a gambler," I said flatly. "I believe in real estate. I've ridden my house up in value for thirty years, more than thirty, actually. That's my nest egg."

"No investments? No cash savings?" asked Norm.

"No. Just my teacher's pension and my house."

Norm whistled. "Zounds, buddy! You are a brave soul."

James winked at Harry. "Brave with a touch of insanity. Just ask his students."

Everyone in the car was silent for a while, thankfully.

It was James who broke it when we saw the turnoff for the casino. "How's the storytelling going, Harry?"

I told him about running into Otto Logan and about my invitation to tell my story at The Cave Comedy Club.

Norm chortled in the back seat. "That place is all has-beens and wannabes. Everyone in the audience is a professional heckler. I wouldn't bother. Just write your book and hope for the best."

By the time we arrived at the hotel, I was ready to turn around and drive back to the boarder, but I couldn't, so I led our bachelor party into the totem-decorated lobby of the hotel. After checking us in, I stepped back as Norm tried using his various membership and reward cards, along with his youthful charm, to pull some strings and get us another room or a bigger one. It didn't work. A national psychologists' convention was happening that weekend, and I had booked the last available room in the hotel. The pretty blonde clerk said that maybe booking the very last room meant it would be a lucky night for us. She gave us each a poker chip and wished us a lucky stay.

"No offence intended," said Norm, "but I'm going to stay up all night and gamble. As pleasant as you all are, I'm not sharing a bed with any of you."

"Great idea, Dad," said James, putting his arm around his father's shoulders. "Let's just use the room to hang our hats. It'll be like the Hawaii Masters all over again." James smiled proudly and pointed at his father's chest. "This man stayed up all night with me and my friends, then got up at five the next morning and won one of the toughest surfing competitions on the planet."

"It's mostly true," laughed Norm.

"I'm up for an all-nighter," said Pierre.

James asked, "How about you, Beast?"

I was tired, tight-chested and wanted to be in bed by midnight so that I wouldn't be too tired for the drive home. "Whatever you want," I said.

"We've missed the comedy show, so we might as well hit the casino," said Norm, slipping a room key in the back pocket of his snug-fitting jeans. He was tall and slim like his son. His grey-blonde hair had a slight surfer shag to it, and he wore stylish, mahogany-coloured loafers with tassels.

Pierre gave Norm a thumbs up. "Let's do it!"

I allowed a small, hard burp to rise and expel itself, but it didn't alleviate my discomfort. My chest and neck felt like they were full of pebbles. As the three men headed down the plush hallway lined with cedar totem poles and murals of ocean scenes, I stood back, knowing I didn't really belong. I felt frumpy, hairy and out-of-sorts.

I called after them, "I'm going to go up to the room first."

James didn't even turn around. He raised his hand and waved.

I stood in the middle of the hallway with clusters of happy gamblers and partygoers stepping around me. I tried telling myself that if Olga didn't want me, I would survive. I had survived Adelle and Cindy. I had survived teaching. I could survive Olga's rejection. I could write my book, sell my house and move to Italy. I didn't have to go backwards. I didn't have to retreat into being miserable. The truth was I didn't want to be miserable anymore. I was tired of surviving life. With or without Olga, I could live it. Couldn't I? It wasn't just the Norms and Jameses of the world, with their pleasant, organized lives and well-adjusted, supportive parents who were entitled to happiness; the Harrys could be happy too. Couldn't they? Even with the wrong mother, the wrong wife, the wrong career, the wrong home, the Harrys could find their way to happiness. Couldn't they? Couldn't I?

James stopped and turned around. He started walking back. I could see Norm and Pierre looking at each other, wondering what was up.

"Do you know what I want you to give me for a wedding present, Beast?" James asked.

"No."

James opened his wallet and handed me his credit card.

"What's that for?"

"I'm begging you to get rid of that beard. Please. For me. For Olga."

Norm and Pierre were stifling their laughter and doing a poor job of hiding it.

"Did she say something to you about it?"

"Just do it."

"It's good advice," Norm added.

James grabbed me by the sleeve and pulled me up to the front desk. The pretty blonde was busy, so James asked an older gentleman who was at the desk if there was a barber at the hotel.

The clerk sized us up and immediately knew who was in need of a barber. "Yes, Sir, we have a twenty-four hour salon, just down that hallway and around the corner." He handed me a business card done up in zebra stripes. "Here is a coupon for a complimentary cut and shave at our in-house salon, Lady Locks."

James was still holding me by the shirt sleeve. "Do you need a chaperone?"

"No," I said, yanking my arm free, "I don't need a chaperone."

Norm and Pierre were wise to stay quiet. I was about to lose it.

"Okay," said James. "We'll meet you in the casino."

"Fine," I said.

"Terrific," said James with a cheeky twinkle in his eyes.

"Fine," I repeated.

Norm burst out laughing.

Thinking back now, I don't blame him, but at the time, I almost turned around and socked him in his surfer smile.

It was fairly late in the evening. The salon was empty. I said hello twice and got no response. As I was about to leave, an attractive stylist walked in from a back room wearing just her bra and panties. Speechless, I handed her the zebra-striped card and let her lead me to her station. As I reclined in the chair, I decided to politely ignore her attire and stare up at the ceiling, which I immediately discovered was mirrored, so I closed my eyes. She had strong hands with a delicate touch and was very nice, chatty and normal, despite being forced to cut hair in her underwear. As I listened to her flirtatious banter, I found myself melting into the chair and acquiescing when she suggested I shave off my beard, rather than just have it cleaned up and styled. When she applied the hot towel on my clean-shaven face, I was actually quite relaxed, my heartburn easing.

When the towel came off, and she started raising the chair to its upright position, my phone rang. It was Olga. I looked at the stylist apologetically.

"You're done, Harry," she said. "Go ahead and answer it. I can see from that sappy expression on your face that you're totally in love with whoever is calling you." She winked. "You can talk right here," she said, patting me affectionately on the shoulder. "Take your time." Then she disappeared into the back room again.

As soon as I said hello, Olga launched into a monologue. She told me she missed me and that she regretted not having made time for me this week. She insisted I come directly to her apartment when I got back, so we could pick up where we left off. I soaked in every sweet sentence, remembering my own love letter to her from Positano. When she finished, I didn't realize she was done, so I remained still and quiet on the other end of the phone.

She filled the silence with, "I think I love you, Harry. I realized it today when I was going from one errand to the next, trying to fill my time. My last stop was the blood donor clinic. I missed my appointment last week at the regular clinic, so I stopped in at one of their mobile clinics, which was in the gym at Dugwood," she sighed. She was almost crying. I could hear her sucking in her tears. "I was the last donor of the day, and by the time I was putting pressure on the needle hole, I was missing you so much. I don't want to do everything alone anymore. You make everything more fun. I love you. I really do. Please come home soon."

We finished our phone call with multiple "I love yous" and "I miss yous," after which I floated across the walkway into the men's clothing store and let the clerk pick out a burgundy Italian dress shirt, an expensive pair of designer jeans and leather loafers, without tassels, for me. I looked good, really good. My face, it looked good too. I was handsome, not hairy. I paid, happily, then floated up to our tiny room, which had a spectacular view of the parking lot. I took a quick shower, put on my new clothes and went down to the casino to join the party.

Then it was noon the next day, and the party was over. I was eager to get on the road. It was a good two-hour drive, plus the border line up, and the others were not moving quickly enough. James was still sound asleep on the sofa with his clothes on.

I stood with a coffee in one hand, my other resting on the thick railing, as I admired the midday view. It was unusually sunny and warm for April. The blue-grey water of the sound sparkled with every breath of wind. The islands were a hazy purple against the bright, clear sky. The tide was part way out, and herons stood in small, stiff-legged groups in the tide pools like watchmen. Sea-soaked logs and driftwood were still jammed up against the coarse grasses and thick shrubs, where the winter tides had left them. A totem pole, taller than the hotel, rose up from the centre of a winterized barbecue area, where chairs, tables and canoes were stacked under tarps that had been pulled loose by wind. The hotel was a massive structure that dominated the inlet. I scanned the empty beach and treed bluffs that stretched south. The view was beautiful, almost as nice as the suite itself. I took a deep breath and exhaled. The gas pains were gone. My doubts about Olga were gone. And, as a bonus, I had an extra five hundred dollars in my wallet, courtesy of the nickel slots.

I had almost fallen off my stool when the blonde from the front desk walked up and handed me the keycard to the Chief's Suite, which had four bedrooms, five full bathrooms, a gourmet kitchen, plush living area, fully equipped bar, and a ten-seater hot tub that could be indoor or outdoor thanks to retractable glass doors. The president of the psychologists' association, who had originally booked the suite, had been delayed, leaving it empty for the night. The hotel manager, who was the same fellow who had given me the complementary cut and shave at Lady Locks, gave the suite to us at no additional charge. James, who was really far gone by that time, had knelt down on the floor in front of me, bowed down, kissed my new loafers, and claimed he was not worthy of such a "greatly-hairy-less-friend." At five in the morning, Norm had declared he had lost enough money for one night, and we had gone up to the suite, where we ate room-service steak and eggs, then crawled into our respective luxury bedrooms and passed out. I had woken up first, showered, then sat on the leather sofa talking to Olga for half an hour with a towel wrapped around my waist, waiting for everyone else to get up so that we could get on the road.

I watched the herons in the tide pools. They were so still, so uncannily motionless. I sipped the last inch of creamy coffee and was about to go inside and try rousing everyone again, when James wandered out on the deck with bleary eyes and nothing but his underwear on.

"What's with you and being pant-less on sun decks?" I asked.

James ignored my remark. "They must have taken about a pound of hair off you at the salon last night," he said, shading his eyes from the sun. "Olga is going to love your new face."

"Well, if she doesn't, then I'm going to drive back here tonight and take that hairstylist out for a drink."

James looked at me. "Yeah, right."

I looked at James, my expression dead serious.

His eyes grew wider. His lips parted, but he didn't say anything.

"All right, I'm joking," I said. "She was pretty and really nice, but she's not in Olga's league."

"Where have I heard that before?"

I found a dip in the silhouette of the hazy purple islands that reminded me of Olga's profile when she was lying beside me. "I'm not in her league," I admitted. "I'm reaching for the stars."

James nodded. "I know what you mean."

9

"Let's go somewhere exotic," said Olga, rolling from her side onto her back and staring at her bedroom ceiling. "I've got some time between gigs coming up. Where could we go that would inspire you to finish your book?" She turned on her side again, propped her head up in the palm of her hand and kissed me. "Can you get away?"

I touched Olga's smooth cheek. "Let me get the renovations back on track, spend some time on the book, and we'll figure something out. I've also got some business with my mother to work out this week."

"Is she getting worse?"

"Better, actually. They're sending her back to Canterbury this week, but she wants me to bring her by the house first."

"So?" Olga asked.

I hesitated, unsure how best to explain my relationship with Adelle. I shrugged and said, "This isn't going to make much sense to you, but she is really attached to the house, even after all these years."

"I can understand that. She probably has a lot of happy memories there."

I chuckled softly and shook my head.

"I love your new face, by the way," she said, touching my bare cheek. "I won't have to worry about allergies or shedding now, will I?" She smiled.

On our way back from the casino, I had stopped at home just long enough to get rid of my thick salt and pepper shadow. "No, you won't…and about those happy memories…there weren't many."

Olga's playful smile turned into a look of concern.

I continued. "So I'm not really sure why she wants to see it, or even why she keeps saying that it's still her house. It's not. You heard the story. That night back in 1981, I signed the papers and took over the mortgage. It's mine. Even Cindy wasn't able to force the sale and take half."

"You know for sure that it's your house?"

"Of course!" I said with an unintended edge of defensiveness in my voice.

Olga nodded with gentle understanding and spoke tenderly. "Perhaps this is just her way of saying she misses your father. I don't see the harm in letting her visit."

How could I explain that taking Adelle for a tour of the half-renovated house would spark a tirade of insults and abuse that I wasn't up to hearing? I couldn't. So I didn't.

Olga pressed, "It can't be that bad."

"I went overboard and knocked out a load-bearing wall, and it hasn't been put back up yet."

"Oh?" said Olga, squinting as she tried to imagine what I had done. "Yourself?"

I nodded.

"How?"

"With a six-pound sledgehammer."

"With a sledgehammer? Yourself?"

"Yes."

"So you really own a sledgehammer."

I stood up and said I did.

She sat up cross-legged on the bed and looked up at me with her head just a little to one side. "So you weren't joking about being a Luddite?"

I shook my head. "I wasn't. I bought it when I was mad that day—do you remember? I sent that email asking you to go on a naked date with me, and I called you a bunch of times, and you didn't call me back—"

"You're blaming me?"

She was upset. Her face was turning red just beneath her cheekbones.

"No. That's not what I meant. I'm not blaming you. It was the same day I emptied my classroom and got kicked off the school grounds. By the time I got home, I was really worked up. I went a little crazy." I paused.

Olga was looking at me oddly.

I got down on my knees, leaned across the bed, took hold of her hands, and said, "I'm sorry."

"It's okay, Harry. I think I understand. It's the toll of living a life you weren't meant to live and dealing with one of the people who helped put you there, one who has been pretty hard on you, I think. Smashing down a wall is…understandable." She smiled and squeezed my hands. "As rough as it was, I'm glad your journey as a teacher brought you to me." She gave me a dazzling smile and added, "And I am very happy to know you are strong enough to put your life on the path of your own choosing. You are being the author of your own existence, Harry. Better now than ten years from now…or never."

I pulled her in for a bear hug. "Let's go back to talking about vacations," I whispered. "Can I take you to Positano sometime?"

"If you do, I promise I will cook for you wearing nothing but my lemon apron."

It felt strange smiling with all that bare skin, but I liked it.

After spending the rest of the weekend, and most of Monday, cozied up with Olga, I was back home, determined to get the renovations moving again as quickly as possible. I wanted the house sold by summer. Carlo and I were standing in the living room looking at the new wall. It had been framed, but it was only three-quarters drywalled.

"I thought the wall would be finished today."

Carlo shrugged. "Tomorrow, it be finished. Then we do floors." His unlit cigarette waved at me as he spoke.

I checked my watch. I was late picking up Adelle from the hospital.

My cell phone rang.

Carlo waited for me to answer it.

I didn't.

"Can we get this whole thing wrapped up by Friday?" I was anxious to get a realtor through to evaluate the place.

"No possible, Teacher. One of my guys no show up today. Drank very much this weekend. We did good job. We finish wall tomorrow, then we start floors. You be happy."

"Happy? I'll be happy when this place is sold."

My cell phone started ringing again. I turned off the ringer.

Carlo raised his eyebrow and frowned. "You got problems, Teacher?"

"Yes, with my mother." I said boldly.

Carlo took the unlit cigarette out of his mouth and pointed at the plywood floor. "This your mother's house, eh?"

"Was her house, thirty years ago."

"The old women, they like old things. They think of the time they were young, pretty. Never changing nothing. Your mother, she not be happy when she see you changing some things. But, when you sell, you get lots of money for reno house. More money. She be happy with you. Mothers, they like their sons to make money." Carlo looked away from me and watched the last of his crew walk out the front door. "We come back tomorrow, Teacher. We finish wall. We start floors." He started following his crew outside.

"Fine," I said, bringing up the rear of our impromptu manly procession, which continued as I got in my hatchback and followed the line of pickup trucks to the end of the block before turning off to go to the hospital.

Traffic wasn't moving particularly quickly, so I used the spare minutes to tap into my storytelling skills and come up with an excuse as to why I couldn't bring Adelle by the house that day. I thought about telling her I was on my way to a teachers' conference and had to be at the airport in an hour. I thought about telling her that the place had been egged and toilet papered by students, angry at me for taking away their cell phones, and that I wanted to fix the place up before she saw it. I thought about saying there had been a kitchen fire when I tried to recreate one of her wonderful roast beef dinners. I thought about just not picking her up at all and telling her later that I had been in an accident.

When I drove into the roundabout and stopped in front of the hospital entrance, Adelle was there in a wheelchair, glaring at me from beneath a blue head scarf. She pointed at me and ordered the nurse to wheel her over to my car. I got out to help and said hello.

My mother, ignoring me but making sure the nurse could hear her, said, "I'm sorry you had to bring Kendal's car. Kendal is my nephew," she lied to the nurse. "He's a pilot. I'm so proud of him." When Adelle's eyes finally landed on my face, I could see she was startled by my appearance. This was her first time seeing me without a beard for thirty years. She quickly recovered. "When will your Mercedes be ready, Harold?"

I thanked the nurse and closed the passenger door. Adelle rapped on the glass and motioned for me to hurry up. I walked very slowly around the car, giving myself time to rifle through my limited ideas, until—I had one, a good one.

"I want to see *my* house, immediately," she ordered when I opened the door.

I sat down, nodded and turned the key. Then I drove around the remainder of the roundabout and pulled jerkily into the parking lot, where I deliberately lurched the car to a stop in a parking stall.

"Stupid, what's wrong with you?"

With a trembling hand, I turned off the ignition and put the keys in my pocket. I clutched my chest and said between shallow, shuddering gasps, "I think...I'm having...a heart attack."

Adelle squinted at me and pursed her lips angrily. "You look fine to me."

"I don't feel good," I said between gasps. "Heart attack."

"I have never seen a heart attack like this at Canterbury. You can't do anything right, can you, you useless twit?"

I dug in my pocket, handed her my cell phone, closed my eyes, and let my head loll back against the headrest. Adelle pushed my phone away, seriously annoyed, took out her own phone, and dialled 9-1-1.

When the operator picked up, Adelle's voice was kind, concerned, motherly. "I need some help with my son. He seems to be having an unusual type of heart attack in the hospital parking lot. It happens with bachelors, you know. Men need the love of a good wife to keep them healthy and strong. He's divorced from a terrible, lazy girl. We are in an orange car of some kind. It's my nephew's car. My son's Mercedes is in the shop."

It took several minutes for the operator to sift through Adelle's monologue and figure out exactly where we were, but, soon enough, I heard a stretcher being wheeled up to the car.

"My mother," I said to the attendants as I was being lifted onto to the stretcher, "she needs a taxi to Canterbury Care Home in West Vancouver."

When I heard someone give the nursing home address to a taxi driver, I had to suppress a powerful urge to jump off the stretcher and take off in my car, but I couldn't really do that. I had to play along until I could politely extricate myself from the situation.

A long while later, Olga walked into my curtained cubicle in the emergency ward. She had just come from some kind of exercise class and looked great in her workout outfit.

"You faked a heart attack?" she said very loudly.

"Sh!" I whispered. "I told you I didn't want to show my mother the renovations."

Olga had both hands on her hips. "Really? This was your best idea? Get her upset by faking a heart attack?"

"She wasn't upset. She was annoyed."

"I don't believe that. You probably scared her more than anything."

"I didn't."

Olga sighed and shook her head, her hands still on her hips.

"Stop looking at me like that. I just had a heart attack. You should feel sorry for me and want to look after me."

Olga didn't move, so I reached over and wrapped my arms around her waist. "Get the nurse, and I'll tell her I feel better. It was just a little heartburn. I'd like to go to your place now."

Olga unwrapped my arms from her waist, plunked them in my lap and said, "Are you sure you're up to it?"

"You can check me over yourself, if you want to."

Olga rolled her eyes. "Did they do any tests when you came in?"

"Yes."

"Then you might as well get the results."

"Bah!" I said, giving her thigh a squeeze. "I'm in great shape. I'm not waiting all night for the doctor to come by and tell me I'm in great shape. Go get the nurse. Please."

Olga kissed the top of my head. "I'll get the nurse." She walked out through the swamp-coloured curtains that outlined my little cubicle. She suddenly appeared again, brightly, and said, "You know, with your haircut, shave and new clothes, you almost had me fooled about being in great shape." She winked at me and disappeared.

"I am in great shape," I called, "best in years."

I reclined against the plastic-covered pillow feeling rather dumb, but, at the same time, I was enjoying the cocky banter with Olga. She had only been gone a few seconds, but I couldn't wait for her to come back.

The curtain was pulled aside sharply. A young male doctor with a shaved head walked in. He pulled up an aluminum stool and sat down next to me. "So, Mr. Tyke, it appears you have not had a heart attack after all."

"I do feel much better now. Sorry about all the hassle."

The doctor shook his head and waved away my apology with his clipboard. "Not a problem, Mr. Tyke. In fact, you've made this a very interesting day."

"How so?" I ventured, sensing something was up.

His expression grew serious. "We've found something."

My cockiness evaporated. "What something?"

"We've found something that, I believe, for a man like you, is cause for some attention."

"A man like me?" I said, swinging my legs over the edge of the bed and sitting up. "What do you mean cause for some attention? I'm perfectly healthy for a man my age." A cloud suddenly descended on my brain, and I blurted out, "This isn't cancer, is it? Don't tell me that. You can't use the 'c' word. I just met the woman of my dreams! You can't give me a death sentence! Not now!"

The doctor shook his head, but his expression remained serious. "What we've found is not as serious as cancer, but it could matter a great deal, especially if you plan to become sexually active." The doctor circled an image on his clipboard and tapped it with his pen. "We've found a marker for a physical condition, a condition that if left untreated could lead to erectile disfunction."

"Are you joking?"

"Erectile dysfunction is nothing to joke about, Mr. Tyke. It can be a terrible strain on a man's state of mind."

"But I don't have any problem getting—"

A suppressed giggle came from the other side of the curtain. I leaned over and saw Olga's bare ankles sticking out of the tops of her hot-pink running shoes.

"You might as well come in," I said.

She stepped around the curtain, beautiful and grinning. "I'm sorry, I couldn't help overhearing." She winked at me or the doctor, I wasn't really sure who. "I'm just happy to hear that you didn't have a heart attack. But," she furrowed her brows and added, "this could have serious implications for your work. Don't you think?"

I had no idea what she was talking about.

She looked at the doctor and said, "He's an adult film star: Harry Willy."

The doctor raised his eyebrows in surprise.

Then she leaned over, picked up my hand and stroked the back of it with deep concern. "You can't retire, Mr. Willy. Your fans absolutely adore you. Just this morning, someone said you have the most perfect—"

"Well, Mr. Tyke," the doctor said matter-of-factly, "then as a man whose livelihood depends on the functionality of his package, I suggest you see your family doctor as soon as possible."

"What is the condition called, Doctor?" Olga asked.

"It's called PND, Penile Nervous Disorder, and one of the most significant causes is long-term obesity. Nerves get pinched in that area from being, well, crushed, if you get my meaning."

Olga burst out laughing. The doctor smiled. And I knew right then I hadn't fooled anyone. I tried to keep it light by saying in a joking tone, "Is this how you tell old men they are too fat?"

"Something like that." The doctor smiled for a moment, but then grew serious, for real this time. "As much as we enjoy having a good story to tell at doctor parties, we don't typically have time for fake heart attacks. Do you understand, Mr. Tyke, or should I say, Mr. Willy?"

"Perfectly," I said, thankful the doctor wasn't writing up a bill for misused medical services.

The doctor stood up. "I'm afraid your clothes have gone missing. We found your keys and wallet, but that's it. You'll have to wear the gown home. Sorry about that." To Olga he winked and said, "You can take him home now." He put his hand out. I took it. "Thanks. It's been fun." And he left us alone.

Olga exhaled. "Serves you right, old guy. That's payback for faking a heart attack. Don't you ever do that again. I was worried sick." She kissed me. "I just found you. I'm not ready to lose you. Not yet."

I stood up in my sock feet and held the back of the gown together with one hand. With the other I hugged Olga.

"What about you?" I asked as we walked down the corridor. "How am I going to pay you back for orchestrating that little scene and for coming up with a name like Harry Willy?"

"By finishing what you've started," she said, leaning her head into my chest as we walked, "everything you've started."

10

I was at The Cave Comedy Club, a low-ceilinged room beneath the Royale Hotel on the east side of downtown Vancouver that smelled like cigarettes, even though it had been smoke-free for three years. Along with James and Greg Logan, Otto's dad, I was waiting, with beer in hand, at a table at the very back of the room for amateur hour to begin.

It had been a good week. I had, proudly, in a fit of all-nighters, put together the rest of my research and finished the first draft of my book, which I titled *Learn, Listen and Tell: Why Teachers Need to Fart in Class Once in a While*. It wasn't a novel—which I still so badly wanted to try my hand at—but I was pleased with myself for actually writing a book, a whole book. I knew the manuscript wasn't perfect; obviously, it needed a lot of polishing, and I wasn't entirely settled on the title, but I felt my arguments were solid, and that maybe I would start a revolution in education, if more than six people read it. Teaching through story could be the next big thing. Full of accomplishment, I had written a scathing letter to the Teachers' Alliance telling them to shove their mandatory twenty hours of counselling and start the paperwork that would get me an early retirement. I had the renovations rolling along at a decent clip. My fake heart attack worked. I hadn't heard from Adelle all week. My hope was that I would have the house sold by the next time we spoke so that when she started up with "my house", I could say "what house?" It had really been a terrific week up to that morning when Norm called me up and offered to pass my manuscript along to his editor for some feedback. Without thinking, I had said yes and immediately drove the manuscript over to his place. At Norm's house, as I was dropping off the manuscript, my face was stuck in a big, goofy smile. But, then, on my way home, I realized what I had just done, and my goofy grin collapsed.

I had promised Olga, sworn up and down, that she would be the first to read the manuscript, but in my excitement over getting professional feedback (with the underlying hope that because it was so good, the editor would take it directly to a publisher, and I would have my first book deal) I had forgotten my promise. Then, instead of waiting to tell her what I had done in person, I blurted it out over the phone when Olga called me from Whistler to tell me she was on her way home from her storytelling workshop. We had had our first tense conversation, and though Olga promised she understood my decision and wasn't really that mad, I feared it was the beginning of the end. Worse, she called me back shortly after that conversation to tell me that the spring rain and heavy snow melt had caused a rockslide on the highway. She wouldn't be back in Vancouver in time to see my performance.

I looked around. The room, which looked like it held over two hundred people, hosted a mixed crowd of older, scruffy, down-and-out individuals. I had expected more of a college-age audience with lots of twenty-somethings who would understand how badly things had gone for my twenty-year-old self. This crowd was nearly my age, some even greyer and more poorly dressed than myself. They looked like the type who had bigger sob stories about their lives than I did. My size fourteens were getting cold.

James elbowed me. "You getting nervous? If you are, you shouldn't. Your story is great. Funny. Wait until they hear about the zebra-striped panties."

"You mean leopard print."

James smiled. "How could I forget?"

"You're getting married soon," I said, glancing around, wondering who else was going up on stage for amateur hour, "so you're excused."

"I think I'm more nervous than you are, Beast."

Greg looked up from his cell phone. He'd been texting since we sat down. "Nervous? Harry's not the one signing his life away. He's got nothing to be nervous about."

I asked Greg, "Am I supposed to go backstage?"

Greg's head was down, still texting. "For amateur hour they bring you up from the crowd." He looked up at me, momentarily, then tilted phone so that I couldn't see the screen. "You'll see."

I let my cheeks and lips go loose as I exhaled. "Now I'm getting nervous."

Before James or Greg could give me a few words of encouragement, the host came out on stage, introduced amateur hour and called up the first wannabe comic. It was a gangly, blonde fellow, really tall, freakishly tall, even taller than me. He reminded me of the spider-man from *The Chrysalids*; his legs and arms were out of proportion for his body. His name was Bert, and I felt really sorry for him. Bert's ten-minute routine about the woes of being a cyclist in Vancouver, in which every second word was f-this and f-that, received one barely audible groan from the crowd, a dozen rude interjections from hecklers, and soured the room. I just kept trying to picture the size of the bicycle the guy must ride. When he was done, there were more boos than applause.

Next up was a middle-aged woman, younger than myself and Olga, maybe forty-five, thin, conservatively dressed, who got some solid laughs for her monologue about parenting in the digital age. I thought some of her jokes about Bill 1010 were quite clever, and that she was good, even if she wasn't hysterically funny and looked quite ordinary. The crowd didn't hoot and holler for her, but she did lift the mood in the room a little.

During the first two acts, people had started to drift in from the casino upstairs. The room was almost full when the host called me to the stage. When he called my name, I froze. James nudged me. Greg looked up from his phone and jerked his head in the direction of the stage. The host called me up again. This time, I stood up and started walking across the carpeted floor, acutely conscious of how soft it was. Some members of the audience were clapping, others were whistling. Someone said as I walked by their table, "Here comes a loser."

When I tripped walking up the stairs to the stage, the host cocked his head in my direction and said, "Here's a guy who terrifies ants and small children."

"Learn to walk, Bozo!" someone yelled.

The host waved at the audience, then looked down at my feet and said, "Ya know, ski season's over, Harry."

There were a few chuckles and smattered, uneven applause

"I give you Harry Tyke," said the host, handing me the microphone and exiting the stage.

I fumbled with my big hands as I tried to put the microphone back in the stand.

"Come on, Big Foot!" a woman shouted from my left.

I looked out across the shadowy haze of faces that were peering up at me from the white fuzz of the bright stage lights. This was a mistake. My story was for my class, for kids in grade six; it was a cautionary tale about what can happen when you give up on your dreams. I didn't think this crowd had ever had dreams. If they did, those dreams were buried under layers of cold, hard sentiment.

"I…" I stopped. This was a mistake. In the empty space between my ears, I heard: What if Olga breaks up with me over the manuscript fiasco? What if she lied about the rockslide?

What if she doesn't want to see me anymore? A vision of Olga sitting at home on her bed, calling me, pretending she was still in Whistler, came into focus on my inner movie screen.

"Loser!" a man shouted.

"He's done!" said a woman.

"Next act please!"

"Next!"

"Next!"

I opened my mouth and said, "It was…"

The crowd started booing me. It was gentle at first, like someone humming, and I didn't mind it. But then someone started a chant: "Next act, please. Next act, please." And the rest took it up. "Next act, please!" I was back in my classroom listening to: "Ugly, hairy beast. Ugly, hairy beast." I felt right at home, only this was better than my classroom. These were adults. Nash Caulfield wasn't there. Mrs. Peach wasn't there. Nor was Adelle Tyke.

I was free.

Fifteen minutes later, I brought my story home by acting out how I had grabbed Cindy by the waist, thrown her over my shoulder, carried her to the back door—all the while trying not to get kneed in the gonads—and dropped her in a lawn chair. I described how when I went back into her computer room, the boyfriend, with a robe on at that point, was shouting and swearing at me, promising to get on the next plane, fly out to Vancouver and kill me. I got down on my knees and pretended to be Cindy, pounding on the backdoor, screaming and swearing at me to let her back inside. Then I was myself, tossing her a change of clothes and keys, minus her house key, out the kitchen window and wishing her well in Chicago.

I said in Cindy's voice: "If you want to divorce me, Harry Tyke, you'll have to give me half this house. You hear me! Half of this house is mine!"

Then I went back into my own normal subdued voice, fished my keys out of my pocket, held up my house key, and shrugged innocently.

The crowd erupted with applause and cheers. The host came out, said a few words in my honour, shook my hand, and ushered me off the stage. As I passed by the tables, people stood up and patted me on the back. When I reached my table, I sat down. James slid a fresh beer in front of me. Greg was up on his feet clapping fiercely and telling me, "Well done! Well done!"

"I'll drink to that," said James, and we raised our glasses and turned our attention to the stage where a guy was riffing on the topic of writing novels. His material was clearly too intellectual for the audience. He was making them think too hard for a Friday night, so even with the wind of my story beneath him, the poor fellow received more heckles than laughs and bombed. When the host came back out, he announced that I had won the night. It was just amateur hour at B-grade comedy club, but it was my night nonetheless. He had me come back up on stage where he handed me a fifty-dollar chip to spend in the casino and a certificate that had my name spelled *Tike* instead of *Tyke*.

When I came back to the table with my award, James asked, "What's next, boys? I think we should do something special."

"I'm in," said Greg, draining his beer.

"I thought you had a set," I said.

"Yeah...but not 'till eleven, and I wouldn't mind killing time at a gentlemens' club. What do you say to a little naked storytelling?"

James and I looked at each other, surprised to hear Olga's phrase coming out of Greg's moustached face.

"No, thanks," said James. Then he stood up, winked at me and said to Greg, "Did you know there is an amazingly hot woman in town who teaches a workshop called The Naked Storyteller?"

Greg, who was putting on his leather jacket, froze with one arm sticking straight out. "I've never heard of her, but I'd take a naked storytelling class. Who is she and where do I sign up?"

James smiled. "Ask Harry. He's one of her students."

Greg grinned. "I see."

"It's not what you think. She's a professional," I said.

"Oh!" said Greg, winking at me. "Don't worry, I get it."

"Not that kind of professional. She's a professional story-teller—forget it! James, you owe me a drink and Olga an apology."

"Too bad," said Greg, unfazed.

"You can have my poker chip," I said, handing it to him, "for later."

Greg shook his head. "I'm a lot of things," he said, "but not a gambler. You should frame it."

I folded up the certificate and put it in my coat pocket along with the chip. I was looking forward to showing it to Olga later and already had plans to give her the chip as a keepsake and officially dub her my muse. It might possibly, I hoped, partially make up for not letting her be the first to read my book.

We walked out through the lobby, laughing and talking about where we could go other than a gentlemens' club. Then, just as I was about to follow Greg and James out the door into the rain, I heard Adelle's voice.

She was in the lobby asking the bouncer, by his first name, to call her a taxi, a nice yellow one, not one of those green minivans.

The bouncer responded with a, "Yes, right away Mrs. Tyke. I'll call right away. Would you like a complimentary beverage while you are waiting? I hear you had a tough night at the tables."

My mother nodded at the bouncer and smiled. She still had not noticed me. "As my Ken used to say: sometimes you're up, sometimes you're down."

She wore a blue sequined dress, with her hair done in a grey square that framed her square, grey face. She had makeup on, a thick layer that was starting to cake and crack, and her shoes were blue and had high heels. On her lap was a blue sequined purse.

"Mother?"

"Good evening, Sonny Boy," she said sweetly with a slight slur.

It was a term of endearment I had not heard her use for decades. It's what Ken had called me when I was a very young, preschool and kindergarten young, when we still lived in our apartment, before the house in Kerrisdale was built.

"When I heard your voice just now, Sonny Boy, it reminded me of Daddy." She opened her blue sequined purse. "Here's a hundred dollars," she said, offering me a crisp bill. "Go have fun with your friends. Daddy would have wanted that."

I snapped the bill out of her hand. "Don't wave cash around in a place like this. You shouldn't be here at all. You should be—"

"Dying of loneliness at Canterbury? No, Sonny Boy. This is the only home I have left, except for my house." She opened her purse again. This time she took out an embroidered handkerchief. "I miss him so much…especially on rainy nights." She dabbed at her eyes.

I knelt down in front of her wheelchair. "I'm going to get you home."

Adelle looked at me and smiled. Her lipstick was frighteningly uneven, her lips dry and cracked. She primly folded her handkerchief and put it back in her purse. She closed her purse firmly and fastened the square, silver clasp. Then she lifted it up and smacked me on the side of the head with it, hard.

I lost my balance and fell back on the floor.

The bouncer was at her side instantly. "Is everything okay, Mrs. Tyke?" he said, stepping over me.

I propped myself up and was about say something about being the one who needed help, but I was interrupted by Adelle. "I'm okay, Max. But would you mind wheeling me closer to the front door. I'm tired."

"Sure thing, Mrs. Tyke."

As James and Greg were helping me back to my feet, the bouncer wheeled Adelle around me and parked her chair by the door.

"What's going on?" whispered James.

"You guys go. I'm going to wait until my mother's cab gets here."

"Sure, Harry," said Greg, nodding at James. And they left.

I kept my distance and watched my mother as she watched the dark, wet street for her taxi. Her purse was upright in her lap and both hands rested on the square, silver clasp. Her nails had been painted with sparkly blue polish to match her dress. They shimmered whenever headlights lit up the lobby.

"There you are, Mrs. Tyke," said a dark-haired man wearing a black suit with red pinstripes and a red bow tie.

"Why, this is a lovely surprise, Mr. Waltzman. Are you here to make sure a frail old woman will live to try her luck next week?"

The manager's affected laughter filled the lobby. "You are a witty woman, Mrs. Tyke. No. I regret I must return to our other very special guests *tout suite*, but I needed to let you know, before you left our humble establishment this evening, that—" The man stopped short. His eyes locked on my silent form. "This is private information, Mrs. Tyke. Would you mind if I took you up to my office?"

"I am exhausted, Mr. Waltzman. Could it not wait until next week?"

The man studied my mother for a moment with his index finger resting on his chin. "As you wish. I will speak with you next week, if you are, *vraiment*, planning to grace us with your sequined radiance."

"That would be delightful, Mr. Waltzman. I will be delighted to speak with you then."

Mr. Waltzman held out his hand, Adelle put her hand in his, and he raised it to his lips, gently kissing it. "Until then," he said sweetly, "*bonne soirée*."

"What was he talking about?" I demanded when he was gone.

"Riding in the rain," she replied, her eyes glassy and focused inwardly.

"What?" I asked sharply. I was losing patience very quickly. The high of winning amateur night was completely gone.

"When you were at school and Daddy was in town, he took me for bike rides in the rain. When we got home, we peeled our wet clothes off in the basement, just inside the back door, and—"

I turned to the bouncer and asked, "Did they say how long it would be?"

The bouncer, who was wider than the doorway, turned his squash-like head to face me and nodded, "The taxi's there. You take care of her, okay? Mr. Waltzman will be wanting to see Mrs. Tyke next Friday."

I forced myself to affirm that I would take care of Adelle. The bouncer came over and opened the door for us. I wheeled my mother outside and put her in the back of the yellow taxi. I helped the cabbie put the wheelchair in the trunk and watched him get in.

He rolled down the passenger window. "Hey! Are you coming? Mrs. Tyke says I have to take her to her house in Kerrisdale. I don't know the address. I only know her usual place in West Vancouver."

"The usual place, please," I said.

The cabbie nodded, rolled up the window and drove away.

11

"Can you believe it?" I said to Olga as I paced her bedroom, waiting for her to finish getting ready for the wedding. The meeting I had had with the director of Canterbury Care home the previous afternoon had left me with a nearly-sleepless night. I had been up, showered, shaved, and dressed in my suit since dawn. Now it was nearly noon, the wedding was at three, and I almost needed another shave.

"Are you still fuming about your mother?" Olga asked from the en suite, where she was still doing her make up.

I stopped pacing and sat down on the bed. "I don't understand where she's getting the money to go gambling every Friday."

"The director called it an allowance, right?"

"Yeah."

"Maybe your father left her an allowance with his estate."

"Maybe. But a thousand a week since she moved into that place? That's almost eight years ago! At a thousand at week, that's—"

"But do you believe the director?" Olga asked from the bathroom where she was putting on false eyelashes.

I threw my arms up. "Why would she lie about that? I'm sure it's the reason they let her go gambling. They're going to make sure she has money to cover her losses." The naked truth suddenly dawned on me. My mother was racking up debt with the casino; the thousand dollars a week was not covering her losses, which is why the manager had insisted on speaking with her the night I saw her at the comedy club.

Olga, with only one eyelash glued in place, came out of the bathroom in a light robe and took one of my hands. "Are you okay?"

I swallowed. "I think the casino has given her a line of credit bigger than the thousand a week. But what did she use for collateral?"

"Probably a trust account of some kind. Or maybe she sold her wedding ring?"

"No. She was wearing it when I saw her at the casino."

"This is all conjecture. Who knows where she's getting the money." She looked at me thoughtfully. "Have you asked your family's estate lawyer?"

My guts were in a knot.

Olga took my red silk tie in her hand, tugged me towards her, then kissed me. "Let's just finish getting ready, okay?"

I nodded. "I am ready."

She smiled at me, kissed me again, then went back to the bathroom to finish up.

"You make a handsome best man, you know," she called.

"I have never seen a more gorgeous Maid of Honour."

Olga laughed. "Matron of Honour. I'm too old to be a maid."

I laughed, even though I didn't agree; the more I came to know her, the younger she looked.

"This takes me back to my wedding day. How about you?" she asked.

"This is a nicer suit than the one I wore back then," I admitted. I said nothing further but moved to the corner of the bed where I could watch Olga apply her lipstick and spritz her swept-up hair. "You are absolutely stunning."

"Wait until you see the dress. Philomena has wonderful taste. No sneak peeks, though," she said. "Go wait in the living room." She walked around me and went to her closet.

I didn't want to go, so feeling boldly in love, I asked, "Do you think you would ever get married again?"

When she didn't answer right away or turn around and look at me, I got nervous and covered up by saying, "My first marriage was a disaster, but I'm older and wiser now. I don't think I have ever truly been in love before. You have shown me a love…I never knew love like this existed…all because of a workshop I was dragged to…"

"Dragged to?" she said, turning around and giving me a mock frown. "You never told me James had to drag you to my workshop. I imagined you had signed up the second you saw it in the conference program."

I was relieved to hear her voice was playful and held no tension. "Can I tell you the truth about something?"

"Of course." She came and sat beside me on the edge of the bed, still in her robe.

"I found it really hard to keep my eyes on your face during our first date."

Olga groaned. "Harry, get out of here so I can get dressed."

Three hours later, and on time, I stood at the front of Our Lady of Sorrow next to James.

"Why are you sweating?" he asked me.

I looked out at the guests and made eye contact with Norm, who was sitting in the front row next to James's mother and grandparents. He gave me a thumbs up.

"Your dad says he has my manuscript back from his editor already, with lots of notes. It's too soon. I'm not ready. And I'm not happy about lots of notes."

"What? You don't think you're the next great social critic, do you?" he whispered sharply. "You're a teacher."

"Yes, I am, and so I know a lot about the education system. Why can't I put my two cents in about what's wrong with it?" I could sense James's frustration level rising, so I backed down a little. "Do you miss eating lunch in my car?"

James's pale face was red, his expression vivid. His movements were jerky and unsure. "Yeah, I do, Beast. Lunch hour is not the same without the infamous Harry Tyke."

"Right," I said, assuming he was being sarcastic.

"Stop being so dense!" said James, giving up the whispering.

The guests looked over at us, so James lowered his voice. "Didn't you read the email from the union this morning? The government has huge support for Bill 1010. We're striking this week!"

I suddenly felt defensive, like James was accusing me of letting him down by making a choice that made me happy for a change. I was annoyed, and it was tough keeping my voice down. "I'm sorry you're starting out married life on strike pay, but I'm out. I don't really give a—"

The music started. Olga was standing at the end of the aisle in her floor-length red gown, which had gathers and tucks in all the right places. The straps framed her breasts and crisscrossed their way up around her elegant neck. Her shoulders were bare, and there was a tantalizing diamond-shaped cut-out in the fabric that made me ache. As she began to walk towards us, I lost all thoughts of James's frustrations, striking teachers and even the feedback on my manuscript. Olga filled me to bursting. As she climbed the steps and took her place on the opposite side of the altar, I was aching to be the one saying "I do."

Everyone rose as Philomena entered with her mother and father. They were small people, each a head shorter than their daughter. They walked her down the aisle, one on each side, and kissed her and hugged her tightly before taking their seats in the front pew. Under her veil, I could see she was crying. I hoped, for James's sake, they were tears of nerves or joy. James's face had returned to a more normal colour, clearly relieved that the bride had arrived and the ceremony was underway.

I winked at Olga, who returned my wink with a dazzling smile. That was it. I was going to marry her. I grinned at her as the priest droned on through the service. We would have a civil ceremony at Vancouver City Hall. She returned my grin with a raised eyebrow and a smirk. Yes, I was going to marry her. Eventually, as the ceremony went on, Philomena stopped crying. She looked very happy, and I was pleased for my friend.

After the ceremony, which my aching knees told me was far longer than the one I wanted to, someday soon, have with Olga, we posed for wedding photos in the church garden. Photos done, the couple took a white limousine to a downtown hotel where the reception was taking place. After showering the car with rice and flowers, Olga and I were ushered to a black limousine, along with the bride and groom's parents.

Philomena's mother, who wore a simple brown dress and small gold hoops in her ears, leaned forward and put her small hand on Olga's leg and said, "*Grazie*. You friend my daughter."

Olga smiled and squeezed the older woman's weathered hand. "She is very lovely. It is easy to be her friend."

Norm smiled as he took us all in. He was flush with pride. "We need to open the bubbly so we can toast to your beautiful daughter." As he reached for the champagne bottle, he added, "And we need to toast to our own Harry Tyke for finishing his first manuscript, too."

Philomena's parents nodded blankly but smiled warmly. Their English was rudimentary, so they didn't appear to understand what a manuscript was. This was the first trip outside Italy for both of them. The husband especially seemed uncomfortable with the language barrier. He turned and whispered something in Italian to his wife.

Norm was handing out champagne glasses. "Bev, where's Harry's manuscript? Didn't we bring it along?"

James's mother, Beverly, was a handsome woman, muscular with a bobbed haircut that ended abruptly at chin length. She wore gold-rimmed glasses that were the same shape as her husband's. According to James and his father, who both constantly bragged about her, Bev was a golfer. She toured with the professional women's circuit whenever Norm's surfing schedule allowed.

Bev turned to Olga and said that my manuscript was in her tote bag.

"Before you get it, Olga, let's make our toasts." Norm raised his glass. "To Philomena, the second most beautiful bride I have ever seen." He winked at his wife. "And to Harry for the start of what is sure to be an interesting literary adventure."

Glasses clinked, then everyone smiled and drank.

After the toast, Olga handed me her glass. She opened Bev's purse and fished out a large, white envelope.

"It's heavy," she said, holding the envelope in both hands. She looked as if she was about to hand it to me, but then she suddenly clutched it to her chest, hesitating, like she was going to say something first.

I waited, painfully, for her to tell everyone that I hadn't let her read it. But she didn't have to say anything. Bev knew exactly what was going on.

"You haven't let her read it yet, Harry," said Bev. "Tsk-tsk. You need to talk to Norm about that."

Norm gave me an apologetic shrug and topped up everyone's glass.

I was holding a champagne glass in each hand, so I shrugged and said casually, "Let me see if it's any good, then I'll let you read it." I thought it sounded reasonable.

Bev and Norm were both shaking their heads. They knew I had said the wrong thing. Olga obviously did too because she dropped the thick manuscript, corner-first, into my lap. The heavy package caught me in precisely the wrong part of my anatomy. I jerked forward, slopped champagne on my pants and yelped.

Olga immediately apologized. Everyone else was embarrassed for me and politely pretended not to notice, except for Philomena's father, who burst out laughing like it was the funniest thing he had seen in his entire life. He guffawed and mumbled in Italian until tears were streaming down his cheeks, and his wife had broken her reserved demeanour and was sternly ordering him to calm down.

I put my arm around Olga and said, "How about if we look at the comments together over coffee tomorrow morning?"

She nodded and smiled but did not say anything.

Looking at the rest of the group, I added, trying to lighten the mood, "...assuming we're not too hung over."

"I'll drink to that," said Norm. He offered to top up everyone's drink for a second time. "By the way did you two book a suite at the hotel for the night?"

"No," I said, "we'll take a taxi home later." I squeezed Olga's shoulders, hoping we were okay.

For the rest of the drive, we talked about Positano and Norm and Bev's recent kitchen renovation. By the time we arrived at the hotel, the mood was much lighter, more appropriate for a wedding reception.

After the ladies and Philomena's father had exited the limousine, Norm grabbed me by the elbow. "I wouldn't let Olga read the comments with you."

"Why not?" I asked, looking at the thick, white envelope Olga had tucked under her elbow.

"The feedback is harsh. The editor said—you'll have to see for yourself what he said."

"You looked at it!"

"Yeah, sure. I was curious. Sorry, buddy," said Norm with a sympathetic shrug. "I thought you'd want to know the truth."

I maneuvered my way out of the limousine to where Olga stood waiting for me with a triumphant grin on her beautiful face. She held out her free hand. When I took it, she pulled me close with surprising force.

She took me aside before going into the lobby and said, "When we were getting ready for the wedding, you asked me something about getting married again."

"Yes," I said, cautiously.

"The answer is, I would, but only to a man who truly trusts me." She held the envelope up as if having it her possession was evidence of my worthiness. "Maybe that's you, Harry Tyke. I really hope it is, because I think a life spent with you would be fun. We could encourage each other, not stifle each other, and definitely not be afraid of disappointing each other when we are trying our best at something that is out of our comfort zones." She tilted her head to one side and looked up at me. "I hope that is you, Harry. I hope we can trust each other, unconditionally love and support each other. So, yes, if I find that kind of relationship, I will marry again."

On the outside, I smiled and gave her a hug and a kiss on the cheek. After all, Olga was open to the idea of getting married again, maybe even to me. But inwardly, I wasn't smiling. Unconditional trust and support sounded great, but were unfamiliar to me, almost in the category of *non possibile*. I had a strong, rising, panic-like urge to be alone when I looked at the editor's "harsh" feedback on my book. I did not like the idea of having Olga looking over my shoulder while my work was torn apart, too humiliating.

"I'm really glad to hear that," was all I managed to say as we followed the few remaining wedding guests inside the hotel.

12

The wedding reception was a bust. The ballroom was luxurious and pretty, with each round table set with red and pink roses and white china, but it was also cramped and stuffy because the hotel's ventilation system stopped working ten minutes after the couple's first dance. I wasn't the only man who had taken off his tie and unbuttoned his shirt; and most of the women's make up was now on the white linen napkins. The appetizers were insufficient for the number of guests. The salmon fillets were dry, the steaks overcooked, the music irritating. The host, James's Uncle Tim, Bev's drunken younger brother from Toronto, made lewd jokes about the bride and was ousted, with James's hearty approval, by four of his cousins. But despite all this, James and Philomena seemed to be enjoying their night. Now it was getting close to midnight, more than half the guests were gone and the band was playing its final set.

I leaned over to Olga, who was turned away from me and having an animated discussion with Philomena about the cost of raising kids in North America, and whispered, "Are you ready to go?"

Olga waved her red finger nails in my face to shoo me away, unwilling to break the flow of her conversation with the bride.

"Excuse me, then," I said, standing up. "I'm going to get some air."

"You can't go now," said Olga, turning around to face me. "I'm taking Philomena to the washroom; she needs help with her dress. You stay here and make sure nothing happens to the manuscript."

She had been guarding the manuscript under her chair like a mother hen all evening.

"You want me to babysit the manuscript?" I said, knowing that was exactly what she wanted me to do.

"The way things have been going tonight, there could be a fire or an earthquake. One of us has to get that book out safely if the sprinklers go off."

Philomena looked alarmed.

"You can't be serious," I said, chuckling.

"Fine. I'll take it with me, then." Olga reached under her chair and pulled out the white envelope. She placed it gently on the table.

Philomena, who was waiting patiently for Olga, said, "Ah! Your book! What is it about, Mr. Tyke?"

I looked at both women. I didn't want to talk about my book, but to appease Olga and be polite to the bride, I said, "It's about education here in North America. I think our teaching methods need to change."

Philomena cocked her head with surprise. "But your schools are very good. James tells me especially here, they are excellent. He is very happy, very proud to be a teacher."

She was cute, endearing. James was lucky. I glanced across the dance floor to where the groom sat with his parents and Philomena's parents, in chairs that lined the dance floor.

Philomena's father and Bev were both red-cheeked, having just sat down after a vigorous dance. Norm caught my eye first, followed by James. They both raised their glasses.

I followed James's gaze back to Philomena and said, "James says our system of education is excellent?"

"Yes, very much so," said Philomena.

Olga looked worriedly at the bride. "Come, let's go to the ladies room," she said, taking Philomena by the elbow and leading her off the riser. Over her bare shoulder, she said to me, "Just make sure the book is fine. And don't look at the comments while I'm gone. Promise!" Her expression was serious to the point of frowning.

"Don't worry about it," I said. "Just go do your woman thing."

As soon as the women left, James and Norm started waving me over.

Judging from the length of corset laces on the back of Philomena's dress, I had at least ten minutes, maybe fifteen, to privately glance at the editor's comments. I pulled the envelope through a maze of candied almonds, tiny bottles of bubbles, rose petals, make up-covered napkins, silver utensils, and half-empty wine glasses. When it was sitting in front of me like a square plate, I used the flat end of a dessert fork to open the flap. I slid my hand inside, gripped the familiar stack of papers and slipped them out onto the table. On top was a single yellow sheet of lined paper with notes on it in red ink. Above the bullet-form notes, in handwriting almost too neat for a man, it said:

Norman. What follows are the top ten elements of this manuscript which must be addressed. Tell Mr. Tyke not to submit the manuscript as is to a publisher. It will certainly be rejected. Extensive revisions needed! Have Mr. Tyke contact me for a quote.

"Zounds, buddy! Put that away!" said Norm, gripping my shoulders and giving them a strong squeeze.

"What was all the waving about?" I asked as I slipped the manuscript back into the envelope, then turned it over to hide the broken seal.

"Ask my son," said Norm. He picked up one of the fuller wine glasses and danced away.

James sat down in Olga's chair. He looked at me with big eyes and a long face. "I'm just going to say it."

"Say what?"

"You can't publish this."

"You read it too?"

"No...sort of. Dad told me about it over breakfast this morning. I needed something to calm me down before I got ready for the wedding...I took it to the bathroom and read your all-for-the-money chapter." He took off his glasses and wiped the sweat off his face.

"So?"

"You can write, you stupid—"

I banged my fist down on the envelope. "Not according to this editor!"

"Well, your writing seemed pretty good to me, but do you—how do I say this?—do you really think I'm in this career just for the pension and summers off?"

I was about to say that I was speaking generally, not specifically about him, but he held his hand up to stop me.

"And I think this hate-on for teachers and the education system comes from your experience with your parents. They forced you to go into teaching and buy their house, which you swear you never wanted to do. But the thing is that under all that blubber and your former-beard is a passion for teaching. I don't know anyone else who cares about the kids more than you do! In fact," he said, using a napkin to wipe the sweat off his face, "I think you love it even more than me. That's why you wrote this. That's why you want to make the system better. Your words say you hate teaching, but your actions say you don't. You have to come back to school. Suck it up. Do the twenty shrink appointments and come back. Tell more stories! Make the change from the inside, starting with your classroom, then write about that. But this," he jammed his index finger onto the manuscript, "just let it be your secret rant. Don't work on it. Don't try to get it published. Come back to Dugwood. Be with the kids. They miss you! September can be your fresh start."

Philomena came up behind James and wrapped her arms around his waist. Olga walked around the couple and came straight to me.

"Thank you for a lovely evening," she said, putting her hand on my shoulder. "It's time to go, Harry."

I couldn't agree more. As I stood up, I held Olga's hand, with the other I waved off the manuscript, which James now held in his hands, offering it to me like a waiter holding a tray of appetizers.

"You keep it. You read it," I said angrily. "Only this time read the whole thing, then tell me what I should do with my life!"

I left, dragging Olga by the hand through the ballroom. Partway across the room, she pulled her hand free and went back, but I kept walking.

I waited in the lobby for her, but when Olga came out carrying the manuscript, I shook my head and went outside.

"Do you want to talk about it?" she asked as we waited for a taxi.

"Are you going to tell me what to do with my life too?"

"You're not being fair. We all care about you. I think James is just worried. He respects you."

I pressed my lips together, shook my head and stared over at an advertisement for a real estate agent at a bus stop across the street. It read: *There has never been a better season to sell!*

"He thinks you're a good teacher. He looks up to you, that's all. But I understand what you want. I understand you, Harry. I really do."

I faced her. She looked up at me with such tender understanding in her soft brown eyes that I couldn't bring myself to blast her. Instead of yelling at her, telling her to mind her own business and let me have the freedom to choose my own career, I asked her a simple question:

"Do you think he's right?"

An unfamiliar look of disappointment surfaced in Olga's expression. She pursed her lips, looked out at the street and said in a subdued tone, "There's a taxi. Flag him, please."

I stepped between Olga and the street. "Not until you answer my question. Is James right? Should I go back to teaching and forget about writing?"

Olga thrust the manuscript into my chest and stepped around me to wave the taxi down. I grabbed the envelope just in time to stop it from falling on the sidewalk. I watched with cold disbelief, and my size fourteens glued to the sidewalk, as Olga got in the taxi without me and left.

It was over an hour's walk from downtown to Kerrisdale, but I felt like I needed a good dose of fresh air and time to think. I followed in the taxi's direction towards the Granville Street Bridge, carrying the envelope in both hands in front of me like a shield. The sky was overcast, but the night was fairly warm, the warmest so far that spring. Within a few dark, quiet blocks, the armpits of my jacket, the seams of my slacks where my thighs rubbed together, and the fabric under my belt, where my roll of fat sagged over, were damp.

By the time I started up the slope of the bridge deck, both heels and one toe were blistering in my stiff leather dress shoes. As I approached the centre of the bridge, I stopped to rest my feet. Looking out at the city-encased inlet, I felt a tightness in my chest. I understood then why middle-aged men sometimes throw themselves off bridges or lock themselves in garages with running cars while their wives and children sleep. When a man realizes his life has gone sideways, that he has sold out for the security, the title, the place to fit in, there just might be no easier, more sensible option than pitching one's bulk off a bridge. I looked down at the water, black and cold, and wondered what it would feel like to jump.

Behind me, I could hear the murmurs of hand-in-hand lovers passing by on their way home from movies and nightclubs. Just ahead of me, three young men were sharing a smoke and laughing at each other's jokes. When they finished their smoke and moved on, I was alone on the bridge. I took the manuscript out of the white envelope, put the yellow paper with the editor's comments in my breast pocket, waited until no cars were driving by, and then unceremoniously dropped the pages off the bridge. A gust of wind held them aloft and even forced one of the pages back up, where it slid under the bottom of the railing and landed a few steps away from me. I went over and picked it up. It was page 57, the first page of chapter five, the chapter James had read, "All for the Money." I was about to throw it over so that it could join the rest of the pages, which stared up with pale eyes from the black surface below. Instead, I folded it neatly and put it in my pocket with the yellow one.

"Look at that!" said a girl who was on her way across the bridge hand-in-hand with her boyfriend.

"Maybe a writer jumped," said her boyfriend casually. "They do crazy stuff like that when they run out of booze."

They stopped nearby, and the girl glanced at me as she leaned over the railing to get a better view. "You're making that up."

"Nope. A lot of writers are poor and miserable and end up killing themselves because they're so depressed," insisted the boy.

"Like what writers?"

"Um...I don't know any names—Oh! The guy who wrote *Conan the Barbarian*. I remember hearing it somewhere. He was, like, thirty or something."

"Really? How did he do it?"

The boy shrugged as he leaned far over the railing. "I don't remember. It's just something a lot of writers end up doing."

The girl tucked her long hair behind her ears. "That's dumb," she said. "But it looks pretty...like cherry blossoms on a wet sidewalk." She grew serious. "What if there really is a writer down there? Should we call an ambulance or something?"

"Nah," said the boy. "If the dude's down there, the dude's dead. They'll find his bloated body tomorrow. What's the difference if he's dead? He doesn't care if they ever find him."

"I don't know," said the girl. "It might be a lady writer. I think we should call someone."

Feeling guilty, I called down to them. "I saw the guy. He just threw his manuscript in the water and walked off. Went that way." I pointed towards downtown.

"Thanks, man," said the boy. He pulled his girlfriend close, and they continued their walk which brought them past the spot where I was still leaning against the railing.

The girl stopped and looked closely at me. "Hey, you're Mr. Tyke. You were my teacher in elementary school...but you had a really big beard, right?"

I didn't recall her face, but I nodded.

"Are you still a teacher?" she asked.

"Sort of."

The girl looked at me critically. "That's your book down there isn't it?"

I looked down at the water. "Maybe."

The boy seemed uncomfortable. "Have a good night, Sir," he said, pulling the girl along. "I hope your next book goes better."

The girl smiled at me and said, "Yeah. Good luck, Mr. Tyke. I hope I see your book in a bookstore someday."

I watched them go. "Me too," I called.

I waited until the young couple was off the bridge and out of sight then followed in the same direction, not looking forward to the uphill climb that waited for me on the other side. The tightness in my chest, which had abated when I let go of the manuscript, was back. I knew tears were coming. I stopped and looked down into the water one last time before the sidewalk veered up Granville Street. I could make out a few white squares on the dark surface, but most were on their way down to the bottom. The first tear squeezed its way out of my right tear duct. The muscles in my chest clamped down on my lungs, making it hard to breathe. I, who hadn't shed a single tear for Cindy or Ken, chastised myself for being such a wimp. I turned away from the water and began the long trudge up the steep hill past shuttered cafés, art galleries, antique furniture stores, and designer clothing shops. With every block I climbed, and every cheery, upscale store I passed, I felt more despondent, the old misery was creeping back in. James had been dead wrong. I had never wanted to be a teacher, did not like being a teacher and certainly wasn't passionate about it. I stopped to rest my aching feet at the top of the slope and pulled out the two pieces of paper I had in my pocket. I tore them up and tossed the pieces in the next garbage can I passed by.

When I got home, I trudged on tender feet down to my basement bachelor suite, threw my wedding outfit on the bar, took a scalding shower, poured myself a drink, sat down ruddy and damp at the card table, and turned on my computer. Without missing a beat, I clicked relentlessly until I was face-to-face with my manuscript. I clicked delete. A box opened up asking me if I was sure I wanted to delete the file: *yes or no?* I moved the cursor over to the *yes* button. One sharp click and all those hours of tapping away happily on the deck of my Positano apartment would be gone.

My index finger brushed the mouse.

I clicked *yes.*

When I realized, five minutes later, that a copy of the file would still be in my trash bin, I went there and repeated the process. My book was gone. Gone.

The sound of a table saw woke me the next morning, but I was exhausted and didn't open my eyes right away. Stupid neighbours. I rolled myself into a sausage in the comforter and put a pillow over my head. There was a loud bang on the floor right above me. I opened my eyes and sat up. It sounded like Carlo's crew, but on a Sunday? I rubbed my face vigorously, grabbed my slacks off the bar, put them on, and went upstairs.

"*Ciao*, Teacher," said Carlo, a cigarette hanging out of his mouth. "We finish floor today. Start kitchen tomorrow."

Two of Carlo's regulars were coming in through the front door with their tools and setting them up in the living room; another was in the kitchen, running a table saw.

"It's Sunday. You said no Sundays."

Carlo pulled the cigarette out of his mouth and pushed two streams of smoke out of his wide nostrils. "No family. No matter. I work Sundays. My wife...yah...no family. Working today."

"Okay," I said, really pleased. "The sooner you finish, the sooner I can get out of here."

"*Si*. House too big for one man, Teacher. You sell. You make money. You buy small house. You live off extra. No wife, no kids, you do good. Retire happy."

"Happy? Are you happy, Carlo?"

"Maybe if wife let me come back to bed."

"What did you do?"

"I lose her book."

"She wrote a book?"

Carlo looked at me, clearly confused. "Not write. She read a book, but no finish. I lose book. She say I no care about her mind, just her body." Carlo looked at the floor wistfully. "*Si*, what a body. She put me on chesterfield."

I couldn't help smiling a little. "Why don't you just go to a bookstore and buy her the book?"

"What book?"

"The book you lost."

"But what book?"

"Oh! I see. You don't know the title. Why don't you just ask her what book she was reading?"

"No possible," said Carlo. "She no talk to me. When a woman no talk to you, you stay away until she want to talk or she kill your balls."

Though I knew Carlo was just muddling his English, I winced at the thought of someone killing my balls.

I went downstairs feeling pretty good about the turn of events. On the landing, I stopped and opened the backdoor. The coach house could use a fresh coat of paint before I put the house on the market. It seemed like a small investment for a big return. I went outside into the cool morning, folding my arms across my bare chest to keep some heat in. Walking to the middle of the unmowed lawn, I turned around and looked up at the siding of the main house. If I was going to do the coach house, I'd have to do the main house too; both needed a fresh coat of white paint, or maybe I'd change the colour. I went back inside.

"Carlo," I called as I jogged up the stairs, "I need a painter!"

Carlo looked up from his pencil and tape measure and said, "*Si.* I have cousin. He very good, very busy painter." With a straight face, the little Italian had the nerve to add, "You want him, you need pay extra just to get him. Understand, Teacher? Five hundred for quote."

I almost went downstairs to get my sledgehammer, which was currently on the bar. Instead, I kept my cool and said, "I won't pay a dollar over the going rate. Tell your cousin, busy or not, we need him. Understand?"

Carlo looked at me for a moment and took a fresh cigarette out from behind his ear. "*Si,* Teacher. I call him."

I went downstairs, took my slacks off and put them back on the bar next to my sledgehammer, and went back to bed. I wrapped myself back up like a sausage in my comforter and tried to ignore the sawing and pounding. I could deal with the renovations and

Carlo's desire to make an extra few bucks off me, but I didn't want to think about last night. No Olga. No book. I was at ground zero. All I needed now was to have my mother show up in her blue dress with shoulder pads and start waving the title in my face and screaming at me about how the house was legally hers.

PART THREE

1

Bronwyn Platt, our family's estate lawyer, was much older than I remembered.

I had only met her once, briefly, years ago at a Christmas cocktail party my parents asked me to host for them while I was still married. They had left New Mexico and flown up so that Ken could see a specialist about his back. I don't remember why the Tyke family lawyer had been invited to that particular party, or why I hadn't seen her since, not even after Ken passed away, but it didn't matter. What did matter was that this woman had all the legal documents concerning the estate and would know how the old lady in blue was financing her gambling hobby.

"Hobby? At this rate!" Platt exclaimed. "Harry, you must be dense. A grand, possibly much more, every week is a full-blown addiction!" The lawyer heaved a large accordion file onto her massive desk and sat herself down heavily. She wasn't a petite woman. The buttons on her suit were strained to bursting, and her face might have been the shape of an olive if she lost a hundred pounds. Evidently, like me, she tried to use her clothes as a girdle; the effect was not flattering.

"You still haven't told me where she's getting the money," I said impatiently. I was very conscious of the time and how much I was paying per minute.

She pulled a fistful of yellowed file folders out of the box. "Keep your shirt on, Harry, while I figure out what I can tell you and what I can't."

"I can see everything, can't I? I believe I have power of attorney when it comes to Adelle—Mother."

Platt stopped and looked at me over her thick glasses. "You were supposed to come in here after your father died and sign some papers, but you never did. You and I should have talked ages ago. We should be good old chums by now, but you never returned my calls."

"I've never been a paperwork guy."

"Aren't you a teacher?"

"My report cards are always late. Anyway, what can you tell me?" I wanted to keep the meeting moving.

She put the files down, sat back in her chair and said, "You seem like a nice kid. So here's what we're going to do. I'll set up an appointment with you and your mother at the care home, and we'll discuss transferring power of attorney to you, and you can ask her, yourself, where she's getting the money."

"Another week could be another thousand dollars or more she'll owe the casino."

"Don't kid yourself. It could be tens of thousands. But she can afford it." Platt shrugged nonchalantly.

"But how? I assume she has a line of credit with the casino. What I don't know is what she's using as collateral."

Platt looked at me again over her glasses. Her soft, puffy cheeks sagged with either disbelief or boredom. I couldn't tell which.

"You know she still owns a big house in the neighbourhood, right? It's worth a couple of million. It shouldn't be a problem clearing up her debts out of the estate sale, when the time comes. You might even inherit a few bucks, if you let her keep having fun."

"What house are you talking about? Their house in New Mexico?"

"No, I said the house here, just down the road, Wiltshire Street." She looked at me as if I was an outright dunce. "They sold their house in New Mexico when they came home to put your father in the hospital. I'm talking about the house you grew up in. She still owns it."

I was livid. "Prove it!" I shouted.

The lawyer looked at me with a pursed, disapproving expression. "I understand you are—"

"She's been saying it's her house..."

The lawyer was shaking her head at me.

"...but I bought it from my father in 1981... September..."

"I'm sorry, Harry."

"...it was raining that night..."

Platt sighed, then dove back into the accordion file, flipped through with deft fingers and pulled out a folder. She went through the papers inside, while I sat there numb and queasy.

"Is this what you signed?" She presented a document to me. Her fat, ringed index finger tapped the place where my signature was.

I nodded brightly. "It's my house. I told you."

She heaved her bossom up on the desk and leaned forward. Snapping her fingers, she said, "Look at me, Harry."

I blinked a few times. My body was heavy, like I was up to my neck in sand or syrup.

"Harry, look at me." She snapped her fingers again.

I looked at her.

"You do know what kind of document you signed, right?"

My lips moved, but no answer came out.

She spoke slowly and exaggerated the syllables in each word so that I would understand. "This isn't a title transfer document. It's a mortgage transfer document. You paid the mortgage, but you don't own the house on Wiltshire."

I thought I saw an aura of black around Bronwyn Platt at that moment. Stupefied, woozy, detached, I watched her sift through more folders and pull out another document. "See, this is the title document," she said, turning the paper around so I could read it. Her hands seemed to move the paper in slow motion, thickly, like her office was full of corn syrup. "The house is legally your mother's."

I had to close my eyes. I bowed my head, eyes still closed.

Platt didn't speak.

I lifted my left hand up to my bare cheeks, pressed my fingers deep into my cheek bones and dragged them down to my chin. I missed my beard. My mouth and my chin were too naked for this moment. Too naked.

"Sorry to be the messenger," Platt said in her upbeat, lawyerly way. "Onwards and upwards."

I opened my eyes. The title paperwork was right in front of me. In all caps near the top of the page, it stated that Adelle Daisy Tyke was, in fact, the legal owner of my house—my house.

The lawyer smiled and kept her tone light. She must have noticed I was imploding. It was pretty obvious. "On the bright side, I think that must have come in handy when you went through your divorce. I remember your divorce lawyer—what was his name?"

She gave me a moment to answer, but I didn't, so she continued.

"I can't remember. Anyway, he called me about the title. I was happy to tell him you don't own title and that your ex was out of luck. Your father was a smart man, saved your family a major financial blow by putting the house in your mother's name." She leaned back, satisfied she had said the magic words that would bring me back to coherence.

My stomach was loose, weak, and my breath was shaking and light. I wanted to cry, but the tears were lodged in my breastbone or in my kneecaps. I couldn't tell where.

"Harry?"

I still couldn't say anything.

Bronwyn Platt got up and opened her office door. "Could we have some Scotch in here please?"

Weakly, I asked, "Now what?"

Platt came over and put a firm hand on my shoulder. "You and I and a title transfer document sit down with your mother and get her to sign it."

The secretary came in and handed me a Scotch. I waved it away, so she put it on the desk. I knew it was a hopeless course of action. Adelle would never sign a title transfer. I put my head down on the desk next to the glass of Scotch.

"We'll find a way to sweeten the deal, Harry."

I looked up at her. "Really?"

"You bet," she said, giving me a hand up out of the chair. "And don't worry about today. My fees are taken care of by a trust fund your father set up. Any business we do related to the family estate is covered. It's probably cold comfort. But don't worry. Worst case, she dies and leaves it to Canterbury or her ladies' auxiliary. But most people don't. They threaten to cut their kids out of the inheritance, but in the end they usually leave everything to them."

As I walked out into the reception area, she said, "Don't look so glum, chum! You've still got a roof over your head. That's better than most."

"Here, Mr. Tyke," said the receptionist, offering me the Scotch again.

I walked out without taking the glass.

Outside, I looked up and down the street for my car. I couldn't see it, nor could I remember where I had parked. I looked up and down the street a second time. Every meter was full. Had I been towed again? I walked up to the end of the block and back again to the lawyer's office. The street was in my neighbourhood, but I was confused. I still couldn't see an orange hatchback butting heads with the luxury sedans and SUVs. I went back to the lawyer's office just in time to find the receptionist locking up.

"Did you forget something, Mr. Tyke," she said flatly, putting the keys in her purse and zipping up the pouch.

"I can't find my car," I confessed.

The girl thought for a moment. "Did you walk here?"

I had walked. I thanked the young lady for her time and the Scotch, which I had not accepted, and wandered towards home—Adelle's home.

That night, me and my size fourteens decided to make up with the woman of my dreams. I had given her the first few days of the week to cool off, but when I got home after the lawyer's I needed to talk to her. Olga told me on the phone she was glad to hear from me, but my instincts, which I now had absolutely no faith in, told me otherwise. I stopped at the flower shop and the wine store, for good measure, and arrived at her apartment in a terrible state.

When she answered the door, my misery and hopelessness grew two sizes. She was wearing a bland, sack-like dress that looked like a painter's smock.

Instead of kissing me right away like she usually did, she gave me a strained smile and said, "I've been worrying about you since the wedding. I'm glad you called."

"Are you?" I said from the hallway.

She waved me in, but I was immovable. "You left me standing like an idiot in front of that hotel."

She shook her head and almost rolled her eyes at me. "Give me those," she said, taking the flowers and wine out of my hands.

I let her have them, then I followed her inside, closed the door behind me and went to the living room. I deliberately avoided sitting down in my favourite spot on the sofa.

"You must be pretty upset," she said, sitting on an antique armchair opposite the sofa, "not calling me for four days."

I shrugged. "Can we open some wine?"

She shook her head. "Let's talk first."

"So talk." I hated that bland sack-dress.

She tried to brighten her expression. "How are the renovations going?"

"Carlo finished the hardwood yesterday. The kitchen cabinets arrived today."

She looked away from me and said, "I'm happy to see you are following through on some things … at least."

There it was. The dig that was going to set things off, but I didn't want to lash out at the bait. That would be too easy. I didn't say a word as I deliberately kept my gaze fixed on the patio door and her container flower garden out on the balcony that was just coming into bloom in spots. I watched the sunset light up the red-brick rooftops of the townhouses across the alley. It was still over a month until summer, but the days were getting longer and brighter.

She broke first and asked me if I thought the house could be sold before summer.

"You mean my mother's house?"

She looked at me, clearly surprised. I ground my molars together. I wanted to tell her everything, spill my problems all over her and let her comfort me, but I couldn't.

"I don't know if I can sell it," I said.

Olga chewed her lower lip with her perfectly white front teeth. "I'm sorry to hear that. How about your book? Did you look at the editor's comments? They were helpful, I hope."

"Helpful?" I said harshly. "You bet they were. They helped me pitch the whole thing into False Creek and delete the file from my computer. So, yes! Very helpful!" I spat out the words. Before she could say anything, I said, "I'm not a writer. I'm a teacher. That's the choice I made, and I'm going to have to live with it forever, which is perfect, because I have just come from the lawyer's office, and it turns out I'm going to have to live with the house, too!"

Olga had tears dribbling down her cheeks. She asked me to explain what I was talking about.

Though I wanted to get up and hug her, I kept my distance; but at the same time, I wanted her to say something, to stop me from giving up, but she didn't. She watched me like I was a car wreck, silently enthralled by my smoking brakes, impaled sides, gushing hoses. I couldn't take her staring at me like she was, with her huge, brown, teary eyes, so I got up to leave.

On my way to the door, I said, without looking back, "You, James, my mother, everyone will be happy. I'm even going to grow my beard back and resurrect my sweater vests."

I was at the door, pretending I wanted to leave. Pretending only. The truth was I wanted her to fix everything: to put my new life back on track, to save me, to welcome me back into the small apartment that had become my home. With a dramatic flourish, I put my forearms up against the door and laid my forehead against my wrists as if I was about to start blubbering. I willed her to get up from the sofa, run across the dinning room, and beg me to stay, then take me to bed and make love to me until I was hopeful.

I watched her closely through the gap between my left armpit and the door. She watched me closely too, and her face was brilliant red above the bland sack-dress. I expected her to start screaming at me, telling me how ridiculous I was, and how I had let her down and was not the man she needed or wanted; but when she spoke, her voice was deep and strained:

"If you really need to leave…go. I won't stop you. You need to be free and happy. It's your life, Harry Tyke."

I lifted my head and took my arms off the door. She had called my bluff. I wasn't going anywhere. Instinctively, I started walking over to her, stepping around the dining room table. She stood up and opened her arms. The bland sack-dress looked better to me at that moment than the red dress with the diamond cutout she had worn to the wedding. I put my arms out. She came around the sofa, threw her head into my shoulder and started to cry. I hugged her tightly.

"Look at how pretty the rooftops are," she eventually said.

She made me smile. "That's why I love you."

"You're going to write a book—a novel?"

"Yes."

"You're going to work things out with your mother and sell the house?"

"Yes."

"You're going to grow a beard and start wearing sweater vests again?"

I laughed. "Maybe." It was my turn to ask questions. "Do you care where we live?"

"No."

"Do you care what I do for a living?"

"I just want you to be happy."

"I am happy," I said, and I meant it.

2

Adelle did not acknowledge me when I walked into her private room at Canterbury. She sat in a chair by the wall-to-wall window, staring out at the saturated tulip beds and dripping evergreen forest, her blue skirt smooth on her lap, her shoulders wrapped in a maroon blanket, and an unlit cigarette resting on the arm of her chair. Brownyn Platt, and the title transfer document, should have been there already. The lawyer had promised to be there an hour before me so that she could start the conversation with Adelle before I arrived.

"Where is Ms. Platt?" I asked.

"Your father used to take me bicycle riding in the rain. When we were in New Mexico, he would say he missed the rain and wished we could fly home just for a rainy afternoon ride."

"Have you heard from Ms. Platt?"

"She was here for a while. But I sent her away."

"What do you mean by sent her away? We need her. There's been a mistake."

She smirked. "I know."

I walked over and stood between the chair and the bed, looking down on her. She still wouldn't look at me.

"This isn't funny. I paid for that house, and we need to transfer the title into my name now. It's the right thing to do. It's what I was promised. Didn't Ms. Platt explain?"

"That doesn't matter anymore. It never did, really." She shrugged her shoulders lightly.

I wanted to shake her so that she'd look at me and have a proper conversation. I said, through clamped teeth, "Stop staring out there. Daddy's not coming to take you bike riding."

She was so still, with her papery, blue-white hands folded on her lap, it was like she wasn't even breathing.

I backed down and tried a softer, more reasonable approach. "Every bit of savings I have is in that house."

Without looking away from the window, she said, "The house is mine, Sonny Boy. I'm leaving it to you in my will...whatever is left." She turned her head just enough to see my reaction and added, "And I don't plan on leaving any of it behind." Then she picked up the unlit cigarette from the armrest and held it to her lips as if to take a drag.

I got down on my knees in front of her and grabbed her hard by the wrists. I twisted both of them, and she dropped the cigarette on her lap and watched it roll down the slope of her blue skirt onto the floor.

Her mouth and jaw were set, tense, but she still wouldn't look me in the face. She said, calmly, defiantly, to the soggy evergreens and water-loaded tulips, "It's my house."

"I bought that house with my life, Mother. I spent almost thirty years of my life in a job I never wanted in the first place."

"And so you should have!" she snapped. "That is what we do. We do things we never really want to in the first place, and we call it a life."

I squeezed her wrists harder and yanked her arms so that she'd look at me. She wouldn't. She let me rock her like a rag doll, back and forth in her chair, half a dozen times, but she wouldn't relent and look at me.

I pulled her arms so that the side of her face was right up to mine. "What did I ever do to you?" I demanded, my throat thick, my voice cracking.

Finally, and I was so relieved that tears started to come up in my eyes, Adelle turned her head, slowly, in my direction. When her eyes finally connected with mine, she said coldly, "You were born."

I let go of her wrists. I wanted to leave and never see her again, but competing with the revulsion was the determination to get what was rightfully mine. It was the same determination Cindy and Mrs. Peach had encountered.

"Daddy owes me that house," Adelle said, her arms limp on her lap. There were bruises coming up on her translucent skin. She didn't rub them or acknowledge in any way that I had physically hurt her. She went back to staring out the window.

"Would you like to hear a story, Sonny Boy?"

"What story?" I said, though I had already heard enough. I got up and stretched the numbness out of my knees.

"About the night I wore my favourite navy blue dress with the shoulder pads."

"I don't really care. I'm going to get Ms. Platt back here to sort this out." I had my cell phone out and was looking for her number.

"It had been a miserable summer. I remember the rain. It was raining hard like it is now. You were up in your room, and I went down to the basement to find Daddy so he could come up and slice the roast. He was on the phone…I found him on it with one of his stewardesses, the one who moved in a few streets away from us that spring. She was married to a lawyer, and they had two young children...do you remember her, Sonny Boy? She always wore her long hair in a high ponytail."

I had already dialled and was waiting for Bronwyn Platt to answer.

"His hands were in his pants," Adelle said as she stared at the crotch of my jeans.

I turned away from her, solely focused on getting the lawyer back and the title transfer signed.

"He was on the phone...," said Adelle softly, "...his hands were in his pants...in my rumpus room." She swatted the backs of my legs to get my attention.

I turned around, and she looked up at me. "It changed everything...that night."

Platt wasn't answering, so I hung up the phone. "What do you mean it changed everything?"

"I told him it was over," she continued, her face tight and expressionless. "I was leaving. We were going to tell you after dinner. I told Daddy to slice the roast while I stepped outside to get some fresh air and have a cigarette." Adelle held up her right hand and pretended to be holding a cigarette between her fingers. She held her fingers to her lips, took a drag and exhaled. "Are those magenta placemats still in the second drawer beside the breakfast nook?"

When I didn't answer, she took another fake drag from her cigarette and said, "Never mind the placemats...then Daddy called you into the living room after dinner. I believed he was going to tell you we were going to get a divorce. Such a liar, a damn liar. He told you a story about us wanting you to become a teacher." She laughed giddily, and shook her head as if it was the first time she had thought it was funny.

She tapped her pretend cigarette ashes into an invisible ashtray she now held on her lap with her other hand. "I never cared what you wanted to do with your life. You could have worked at a video store or joined the navy. I didn't care. I thought you were on the right track at that little newspaper. You were out of the house all day, out of my hair. That was enough. But Daddy, he made it all up. Such a storyteller."

I backed away from her until I ran into the bed. I sat down heavily and looked right at her not knowing who the storyteller really was. "But you must have known he was going to sell me the house…there were papers…he had a pen."

Adelle shook her head. "I just played along. Pretty convincing, wasn't I?"

I stared at her, speechless.

"I thought living in a faraway desert would bring Daddy back to me...it did, for a time…"

She smiled, but not at me.

"But the papers I signed that night, where did they come from?"

"You signed mortgage renewal papers the bank had given to Daddy that morning. Trust me, there was no thought behind this. He made it all up faster than he zipped up his fly when I caught him on the phone with that—"

"So he was never going to put the house in my name?"

"Yes, he was," Adelle said brightly, "but I told him he couldn't, that I'd leave him if he did." She emphatically ground out her fake cigarette in her pretend ashtray.

Three strides across the room, my sledgehammer-wielding hands around her papery neck, and the house would be mine. Wasn't that what Bronwyn Platt had said? And Adelle herself just moments ago? It would be mine when she was dead.

I walked out, then, with Adelle still talking at me, telling me a story, her story, about what happened that Labour Day Sunday in 1981.

"I needed to make sure that if that liar ever left me I would be taken care of. I made him transfer the title into my name–and he did!"

Disturbed and despondent, I arrived home just as Carlo and his crew were packing up for the day. As Carlo jogged down the front steps with a ladder on his shoulder, he gave me a big grin and said, "Teacher, I need to talk about my cousin the painter and the other things."

It was still raining hard, so I went up and waited on the stoop for him.

Carlo walked up with an unlit cigarette between his lips. "So my cousin's painters can start tomorrow. Okay?"

"I have no money," I stated.

Carlo pulled the cigarette out from his lips. "What you mean you have no money? You no pay me what you owe me?"

"I'll pay you, but there's no money for exterior painting or the new main floor powder room. Just finish what we started and give me the bill." I looked down at Carlo's paint-spattered work boots and shook my head. "Tell your cousin...well...whatever you want. I can't do it. I'm out of money."

Carlo lit his cigarette. He inhaled deeply and said, "Ah! I see. The old women, they no like change. But you still sell the house, no?"

"I can't."

"No possible?"

"No possible," I said, turning to go inside.

Carlo shrugged and took another drag. "We finish this week. We leave you to your life, Teacher. It's nice house now. You be happy. Your mother be happy too. Looks very nice, very good."

He was right. The house looked really nice and good. I had spent a lot of money that I had hoped to recoup when the house sold.

"Maybe she come live with you again, eh? She have accident on stairs, maybe bump the head, then you call me. We finish everything, and you sell your house, get top dollar. You go to *Italia* with your woman. You write, eh? Just little accident, then everything possible." He laughed heartily. "Forgive me, Mama," he said to the rain clouds.

I was already in the foyer. I looked over my shoulder at the little contractor. "I don't think so, but thanks. You've done a great job. The place looks good."

He saluted me with the hand that held the cigarette. "*Ciao*, Teacher. We see you tomorrow."

When he was gone, I went back out on the stoop. I bent down and swept away the wood dust and chips of paint with my hands. Then I sat down with my legs wide open and my size fourteens planted heavily on a step. I couldn't remember sitting there like that since I was a boy, waiting for a rare glimpse of my father who would pull up in a yellow taxi, dashing and cocksure, in his pilot's uniform.

My pants were getting wet from the knees down, but I didn't care. Wet pants were nothing. I exhaled and ran both hands over my bowed head. I had given up my dreams to help "Daddy" make up with Adelle, and I had been too stupid, too numb, to notice that it had all been for nothing.

I looked up and down the street. The heavy spring rain gave the emerald greens of the lawns and emerging gardens a thick, glossy sheen that reminded me of Olga's red high heels. It was mostly quiet except for the rain pattering on the gable above me and the occasional whoosh of a car driving through puddles.

My cell phone rang. It was Olga. I answered curtly and the battery died. I hadn't meant to be rude, I just was at the moment. I stood up. I'd have to go inside and call her back on the house phone. I stood on the threshold of the open front door taking in the renovated foyer, living room, and what I could see of the kitchen. The place looked great. It would sell easily and might even drive a bidding war. But what did it matter? It had been all for nothing.

The house line was already ringing when I reached the top of the basement stairs. Knowing it was Olga, I was about to run down to catch it before the last ring, but something stopped me. Leaning against the wall by the backdoor was my six-pound sledgehammer. The phone stopped ringing, and I descended the stairs quickly, knowing I needed to call Olga back.

On the landing, I stopped and picked up my sledgehammer. It felt good in my bare hands. Slinging it over my shoulder felt even better. I turned and walked back upstairs. I looked around for something that would take my hammer blow well, something that would explode and cover me in shards of debris. I pivoted on my heel, the sledgehammer still resting on my shoulder, and walked into the sleek new kitchen. The massive pantry cabinets needed to be shuffled to their final resting place around the new stainless refrigerator, a few handles needed to be installed and the crown moulding needed to be mounted, but otherwise it was nearly done, nearly perfect, very nice, very good.

I stopped in front of the island and lifted the hammer off my shoulder. I loved the weight of it in my hands and for a moment wondered why I had never considered a career in the trades. Holding the hammer made me feel like a man should feel: ox-like, fearless, capable.

I locked my gaze on a pale splotch in the pattern of the black and grey marble countertop and wound up to swing.

"What you doing, Teacher?"

I paused but didn't turn around.

"You kill you mother, not the kitchen. What the kitchen do to you? She love you."

When I still didn't turn around, Carlo said, "Bah! Do what you want! I forget my thermos. My wife kill my balls when I forget. You pay tomorrow. Okay? *Ciao!*"

As soon as the front door shut behind Carlo, I put the sledge-hammer down on the countertop and braced myself on it. My triceps ached to pick up the hammer and swing. I wanted to prove to myself I could smash through anything with a single blow.

The phone rang again. I pushed myself back to my feet, grabbed the sledgehammer and jogged downstairs. I tossed the sledgehammer on my unmade bed and answered. It was Olga. She was on her way over with news. I was not in the mood for news, but I wanted to hold her.

3

I stood in line at Jitters waiting to order. I flinched when a woman came in and shook her umbrella out on me. "Nice," I mumbled, running a hand along the back of my jeans.

The woman shrugged and plunked her umbrella in the plastic stand by the door.

During the early hours of the night, as I dozed with Olga wrapped securely in my arms, the local rain makers held a union meeting and decided they needed to step up their efforts and make a statement. Even for Vancouver, this was crazy. It reminded me of one morning in Positano when James and I had watched a torrent run down the steps outside the apartment door. We had joked about it being like living in a giant toilet bowl that's just been flushed. I was glad I wasn't going to be on the picket line all day.

After I almost took my sledgehammer to my brand new kitchen, or, should I say, Adelle's brand new kitchen, Olga had come over and spent the rest of the day with me. Her big news had been asking me to teach with her in Mexico over the summer. She had jobs lined up for both of us that would last through November. I had given her my own big news: that I hadn't been able to work things out with my mother and the lawyer and, therefore, had to do the twenty hours with Richard Petersen and get back to teaching full-time as soon as the strike was over. The next day, Principal Caulfield had called me and said he needed help with the students who were still being dropped off every day despite the strike. I would get overtime wages, if I crossed the picket line to help out. How could I say no?

"Hey, Beast," said James, who was just coming out of the Jitter's bathroom. "This reminds me of Positano. Can you order for me?"

I hadn't seen him since the wedding. He looked thinner, if that was possible.

"You're here early for a man of leisure," he teased. "What are you up to today: supervising high-end renos and editing that book of yours? Life's rough, eh?"

"Nice outfit," I said, nodding at James's bright orange rain slicker and matching rubber pants.

He adjusted the thick plastic collar. "I bought this at a fishing supply store. Good thing, too. It's even worse this morning than it was yesterday. Being wet on the line is a nightmare."

I chuckled when James pulled up the hem and showed off the matching rubber boots.

"I know I look like a salmon farmer, but at least I'm dry."

I stepped up to the counter and bought our coffees. James waited for me at the cream and sugar counter, which was near the door. I walked up and passed James his coffee. "What time does the picket line open?"

James frowned. "What do you think it is, a drug store? Someone's got to man the line around the clock. The school has been getting scabs through. That stops today. We've got special ammo for scabs." He winked.

"Scabs? I can't believe you just called another human being a scab. You're taking this whole thing too seriously."

"It is serious," said James as he opened the door for the woman who had shaken her umbrella out on me. "You didn't read her book, did you?"

"Who's book?"

"Remember at the conference you skipped out of a workshop about strikes to come with me to Olga's workshop. The speaker, Gretta Hagride, she wrote a book about surviving on the picket line." James got a strange look on his face. "How is it going with Olga, anyway? I heard she left you at the reception and took a taxi home on her own. Have you patched things up?"

"Of course," I said. "I'm old, not stupid."

He laughed. "So, anyway, some of the go-getters at Dugwood took that workshop with Hagride. Then just after you quit, or whatever you want to call it, they decided to use the teachers' lunch fund to buy a copy of the book for everyone. Gretta is giving the proceeds of her book sales to the One Laptop Per Child Program, and her book is really good—good advice about striking and what to bring to a picket line to make it fun, sort of. There's a copy for you in your mailbox in the office, but I don't imagine you'll be able to pick it up any time soon."

"So you read this woman's book, and now people who want to cross the line to help out with the students, who are being dropped off at the school by parents who don't have other options, are scabs? That's pretty harsh—especially for you!"

James's expression hardened. "Actually, harsh is telling your new wife the honeymoon is postponed, maybe even cancelled, because the government has decided teachers have no real value. That's harsh."

"Did Philomena kill your balls?"

"What are you talking about?"

"It's an expression my contractor uses."

James shook his head. "Must be nice to have it all figured out. Enjoy editing your book and hanging around all day with your woman in your newly-renovated, multimillion dollar home. I'm late for my shift." Emphatically, he pulled his orange hood over his head, turned his back on me and walked out.

"Wait! James!" I put a lid on my coffee cup and chased him out the door. "James!"

He was already in his blue SUV and backing out. When he came to a stop in the line of cars waiting to pull out onto the street, I banged on the passenger-side window.

"What? I'm late!" said James, rolling it down.

"I just wanted to tell you...I'm crossing the picket line."

"When?"

"Now."

The driver behind James honked.

I waved at the driver and gestured that I needed another minute. "I need the money."

"Why?"

"I'll tell you later. Just make sure I don't get egged or hit with whatever it is you've got for ammo today."

"This isn't funny, Harry. How can you be a scab? You don't even teach anymore."

"Just tell them not to egg me, okay?"

James shook his head. "I don't know..."

A driver in a silver sedan, who was trying to turn into the parking lot, honked aggressively.

"I've got to go. I can't promise you'll get across," he called as he peeled out of the parking lot, the rain still pelting into his vehicle through the open passenger window.

I ran to my car, doing my best to keep my running shoes out of the puddles. I jumped inside, soggy right through, and jammed the cup into the holder. I squealed out of parking lot to catch up with James.

Scab. I didn't even know what it really meant or why that's what you call someone who crosses a picket line. I was also choked that the money in the teachers' lunch fund, which was largely raised by the selling of baked goods of which I had been a huge supporter, had been used to support the One Laptop Per Child Program. Stupid to give more kids more computer time. Stupid to replace teachers with digital education. Idiotic. I wished I could just pick up and go with Olga to Mexico and teach for as long as we wanted. She had something like her previous naked classroom scenario set up. It would be all about the stories and connecting with the kids without technology, without teaching aids and without props. It sounded like heaven, if only I could afford it. I lifted my right hand and banged it down on the steering wheel, then turned the windshield wipers on high, banged the steering wheel again, and sped up to catch James. I could see his taillights stopped at the next set of traffic lights. But before I could catch up, he turned off the main road onto Dugwood Lane. I followed him around the corner and straight into a triple row of black and white traffic barricades. I could see James parking up ahead in the school parking lot and suddenly realized that being a scab, ridiculous as it seemed to me, was not going to be easy.

I was forced to stop my car. Marigold Lovitt tapped on my window with chill-reddened knuckles. She wore a yellow slicker and boots like James, and a placard that read: *Bill 1010 is the END.* Someone had turned the zeros in 1010 into nooses.

I rolled down the window and decided to play dumb.

Marigold smiled. "Well, good morning, Harry Tyke. How nice of you to come out and support the cause, even while you're on leave."

I moulded my expression into a sweet look of resignation. "I wish I could stay and help out, but I can't. You've go to let me through, Kathy. I just need to pick up a few things from my desk and clear out my mailbox."

"Can't do it, Harry. No one comes through except the union members running the picket line and our wonderful parent supporters like Mrs. Peach over there. I'm going to have to ask you to turn your car around and head home so we can get this morning's shift parked and on the line."

"Mr. Tyke! It's Mr. Tyke!" shouted Otto Logan from the sidewalk. He and his dad were half-hidden under a large umbrella. Greg waved at me.

I nodded, then looked at Marigold Lovitt. "Fine. I'll turn around."

I pulled a tight, aggressive u-turn, squealing my tires, and parked behind Greg's family wagon, which was just up the street. As I got out, I saw James walking over to the counsellor in his orange slicker. Mrs. Peach was there with a handful of other parents. They were handing something to the teachers. It looked like tomatoes, which seemed odd, but I couldn't be sure that's what they were.

Greg came up to me and stuck out his hand. "I thought you were out of teaching now," he said.

I accepted his hand and shook it. "I thought so too, but fate has a funny way of killing your balls sometimes."

"You've got that right." He gestured at the picket line where a dozen teachers now stood with rain spattering against their placards. "Are you breaking the line?"

I looked over at James, who was looking back at me through the rain. "Yeah, Caulfield needs some help with the students and—"

Otto jumped up and down, clapping his hands. "Mr. Tyke is telling stories! Mr. Tyke is telling stories! Shoulder pads! Shoulder pads!"

Greg put a firm hand on his son's shoulder to settle him down. When Otto was quiet, Greg said, "Do you think I'm a crappy father?"

I looked at Otto, who was still whispering to himself about shoulder pads. "I get it. You need to—you've got to earn a living. And so do I."

Greg looked at me. "Let's do it."

"How have you been getting Otto through every day?" I asked as we started walking towards the picket line.

"This is our first day back. We've kept him home as long as we could."

"Oh," I said. I looked around to see if other students were being dropped off. There were none. The only other people on the block were the strikers and the supporting parents, who were now lined up along the barricades, shoulder to shoulder, with their arms linked at the elbows. They weren't saying anything or throwing anything, yet. Dribbles of water seeped through to my hair follicles and down the back of my neck and around my ears.

I shook my head to get some of the water off, then looked at Greg and said, "Follow my lead."

He nodded. Otto stared at me, his eyes wide with expectation and a huge smile on his face.

"Let's get you to class, Otto."

"Okay, Mr. Tyke," said Otto confidently.

Greg and I continued walking, side by side, along the sidewalk towards the line of rain slickers and placards. Otto stayed two steps behind us. Greg held the huge umbrella over us like a shield.

"Stop there, Harry!" shouted James from his position in the middle of the line. "You're not crossing today. You too, Mr. Logan. Take Otto home. School's closed."

We kept walking along the sidewalk, right at the barricade.

"Bill 1010 is the end! Bill 1010 is the end!" chanted the teachers and parents.

Two teachers, arms linked, shuffled the entire line over to the sidewalk to block us.

I stopped walking when I was just a few feet away from the line and faced two former colleagues—Sharon and Kelly, both kindergarten teachers. I was a foot taller than the two of them put together.

"Are you going to make me pick you up and move you out of the way? Trust me, I will. You can ask Mrs. Peach down there. She'll tell you that I've got no problem moving tiny obstacles out of my way."

They frowned at me and continued chanting: "Bill 1010 is the end!"

"Watch yourself, Harry!" shouted James. He was six bodies down the line. "You'd all better go home. No one is crossing. Not today. Sorry, Otto."

Otto, looking very distressed, was about to start melting down.

"Listen, Otto," I said. "You are going to school today and so am I."

I left Greg and Otto on the sidewalk and stepped out onto the street. I walked down the line and stopped in front of James. He looked so foolish in that rain slicker, like a skinny kindergarten kid. His glasses were spattered with rain.

"We are doing this for kids like Otto, Harry. They need fully qualified teachers in the classroom, not teaching assistants."

I sniffed with disbelief, then exhaled forcefully, sending a wild spray off the end of my nose. "That's a very convincing story you're telling yourselves," I said, wiping the rain off my forehead with my trench coat sleeve and upping the volume of my voice so everyone could hear me. "But let's be honest. Being a glorified EDDS babysitter at your current salary while the kids are gaming out all day in the classroom is a sweet gig. I'd understand completely—if I didn't think that screen-centred parenting, and now screen-centre teaching, weren't both so low."

"You don't understand anything about teaching or parenting!" keened Mrs. Peach from the end of the line. She yanked her end closer so that I was starting to become encased in a rubberized human horseshoe.

I stepped back from James and faced her. She was decked out in an expensive, open-water survival suit. Since she wasn't on a deep-sea fishing boat she looked ridiculous. I could barely see her face under the visor of her pinched hood.

"Is that right?" I said.

"Nothing good," she scowled.

I put my hands on my hips and wiggled them. Then, imitating Alexa imitating her mother, I said:

"You can't play social games anymore, Alexa. I don't want you meeting a bunch of questionable strangers on the computer."

"You're a menace, Harry Tyke. I'm sorry I dropped the lawsuit," said Mrs. Peach.

"So am I," I challenged.

"Arm the tomatoes!" shouted Marigold Lovitt as she unlinked herself from James and ran behind the first barricade.

The line broke and ran to where Marigold was handing out tomatoes from the plastic crates that were used at the school on fruit and vegetable days.

"Do you people have any idea how ridiculous you look?" I said to all of them.

Mrs. Peach shouted, "Scab!" and threw a fat, hothouse tomato at me. It splattered on the road beside my runners.

"Go home, Harry," said James sternly. He cradled a large ripe tomato in one hand.

Behind me I could hear the sound of cars turning around as newly arrived parents saw the seriousness of the picket line and resigned themselves to making other childcare plans or missing another day of work.

"I'm not going home, James." I pointed to the sidewalk where Greg and Otto watched silently. "I'm taking Otto to school today, and we're going to tell stories. Want to join us?"

James cocked his arm and aimed his tomato at me. "No one is going to school today, Beast. No one."

"James!" I laughed. I just couldn't hold it in anymore. "Bill 1010 is not going away because of a crate full of tomatoes and a bunch of fisherman-look-a-likes. It's how we raise our kids now. No one is really against it, not the teachers, not the parents, not the administrators. No one here really cares about the real problem with Bill 1010...except me."

James took a step towards me. I thought he was going to bean me with his tomato, so I flinched and ducked a little. The other teachers cocked their arms too and aimed their tomatoes at me. Several picketers shouted, "Scab!"

"James! If the average parent logs more than four hours a day gaming and lets their kids have unlimited screen time so that they can game in peace, why do you think you can stop the same thing from happening in schools? Do you know why? Because for you, this strike isn't about the insanity of letting computers raise our kids; it's about jobs. Right? It's not about the kids. It's about the salary, the benefits and the security of a government pension. Trust me, it's about the money. I know it is. It's my story too..."

"Scab!"

"Scab!"

Big surprise. They didn't get it. I turned my back on the line and their tomatoes and walked down the road to my car. There was a collective cheer behind me, accompanied by Otto, who was screaming at me to help him. I looked over at the boy, who was being restrained by his father, his young face in agony and eyes wild with anger. I knew he was ready to explode in a burst of fist-filled fury. I winked at Greg and Otto. Otto didn't see me wink, so Greg whispered something in his son's ear and pointed at me. Greg nodded, gave me a thumb's up, and held on tight to his son, who was breathing hard and straining to be turned loose. I opened the hatchback and took out my six-pound sledgehammer.

"What are you up to, Tyke?" said Nash Caulfeild, walking over.

I looked at the principal's clean, dry face and starched, white collar. "I'm going to break a picket line. You might want to wait here."

I shut the hatchback gently and hefted the sledgehammer in both hands. "Do you have something to say to me, Nash, another lecture about how I'm cocking things up, how they will definitely want my head, how I'm jeopardizing Dugwood's reputation for being a respectful place to learn? Have you got something like that you'd like to say to me?"

The principal's face paled slightly.

I smiled. "Well, then, we understand each other."

I tested the weight of the hammer in my hands, turned, and winked again at Otto and Greg. Then I strode towards the picket line, increasing my speed and lifting the hammer higher over my head with every step. Behind me a crowd had gathered. Optimistic parents and grouchy students were all watching as the big, hairy teacher, Mr. Tyke, who they called Beast, ran at the row of rain slickers and black and white barricades, wielding a sledgehammer like a caveman.

"Arm your tomatoes!" cried Mrs. Peach. "He's a menace!"

"Fire!" shouted Marigold Lovitt.

I was pelted with tomatoes in the chest and legs. They were annoying, but they didn't slow me down. When I was within a few arm lengths of the first barricade, I growled and swung my sledgehammer. The barricade broke into several chunks of wood that landed in deep puddles.

Some of the teachers on the picket line were shouting "Scab!" Others were shouting "Run!" Others were arming themselves with more tomatoes and eggs now, too, and were pelting me with them as they retreated behind the second barricade.

Over the din and the rain, James shouted. "Harry, stop or we'll call the police!"

In response, I wound up and smashed the second barricade into three big pieces and kept running into the flying produce, dodging the near misses and name calling.

I heard Otto shout, "You should have shoulder pads!"

As I approached the third barricade, I put the head of my sledgehammer on the ground, looked at James and said, "It all comes down to the naked truth, doesn't it?"

The rain had slowed.

James pulled his hood off. "What truth?"

"Did you mean what you said at the reception?"

James looked at me blankly. "About what?"

"About my book and about coming back and changing things from the inside. Did you mean that?"

James stared at me for a moment, then nodded.

I looked at my friend in his orange slicker and said, "Then let me start today."

"Arm the tomatoes!" shouted Mrs. Peach.

I picked up the sledgehammer and lifted it over my head.

"Let them through," said James.

"Who says you're in charge?" said Marigold Lovitt and Mrs. Peach at the same time.

"Harry does," said James.

They all looked at me and put their tomatoes and eggs down.

I put my sledgehammer on my shoulder, went over to the sidewalk and said to Greg, "You can go. I'll take Otto to class."

Greg shook my free hand. He looked like he was holding in tears.

"What's wrong?" I asked.

Greg just shook his head, knelt down and hugged his son.

I kept my eyes on the picketers as the principal, followed by the other parents who needed to drop off their children, came over to where Greg had Otto locked in a bear hug.

"Come on, Greg," I said touching his arm, "school's in."

Greg looked up at me and said with deep sincerity, "Thanks, Harry. I'm proud to have you as my son's teacher."

I smiled at him. Then, with my sledgehammer comfortably resting on my right shoulder, I led the students into the school.

4

It was raining, nothing newsworthy for Vancouver in February. I stood under the grimy plexiglass entryway of Sundry Tech, the biggest and most modern high school in the district.

It was a Friday, nearly Valentine's Day, and the first professional day of the new year. I looked down at the conference brochure which was open to the page containing the blurb about my morning workshop: The Naked Storyteller.

Before there were books, there were stories—stories told without computers, tablets or televisions—stories specific to one's landscape, language, culture, and values. Awaken your inner storyteller in this candlelight session as we share secrets from the ancient art of storytelling. By the end of the workshop, participants will be equipped to teach through storytelling, using just their voices, bodies and imaginations.

I checked my watch. It was eight thirty-five. I could see through the glass doors that the foyer and cafeteria were rapidly filling with teachers—one or two smiling and chatting excitedly, some looking for a caffeine fix, others on their way to the toilet or to have a smoke before the keynote address.

"Sorry I'm late," said Olga, coming up to me and giving me a kiss on my bearded cheek.

I kissed her on the lips and admired her three-carat diamond engagement ring. It was a solitary diamond almost as wide as her slender finger, and it sparkled beautifully no matter how she moved.

"Never mind me," I said, opening the door for her and watching her walk inside wearing her glossy red high heels. "Did you get ahold of Rally after I left this morning?"

"Yes."

"And?"

"He's agreed to sign the divorce papers, and—"

Olga stopped at the registration table to find out what room our workshop was in. Then she walked off in a hurry across the foyer without finishing her sentence.

I followed as she silently, and seemingly deep in thought, rounded a corner and walked briskly down the corridor towards the drama room. I tried to be patient, but I couldn't wait any longer. "And what?" I asked abruptly.

Olga found our classroom and opened the door. "Can you get me some coffee? Black with a few grains of sugar please."

"Sure," I said, not liking the suspense. I didn't trust Rally. Since he had found out Olga wanted to remarry, he had been trying to woo her back with flowers, jewellery and exotic trips. He even offered to buy her a sports car and a penthouse apartment downtown. Of course Olga had openly rejected him and declined every gift, but it bothered me, deeply, that the divorce papers were still not signed.

Familiar faces smiled and looked at me with curiosity as I passed by them on my way back to the foyer. I nodded and tried to smile back, despite the feeling in my gut that something was up with Rally. What was Olga not telling me? After the strike last year, Rally had written a series of sensational articles about my exploits on the picket line and in the school during the short-lived strike. With a mixture of admiration and resentment, my fiancée's ex-husband had turned me into a celebrity teacher in the community—the "beast" with a heart for stories who saved his students, not from Bill 1010, which passed and was signed into law the week before Labour Day, but from those digital evils, like laziness and zoning out that we like to tell ourselves we are against but really aren't.

When a local publishing house caught wind that I was working on a book criticizing the education system, they made me a deal and told me to be provocative. They gave me a two thousand dollar advance, which Olga and I put towards a writing desk in her apartment last fall. Adelle had passed away, unexpectedly, early in the summer, ironically, while visiting *her* house on the last day of June. We were in the newly-renovated living room, and she was riding me about the whereabouts of her cuckoo clock, when she hit her head on a blunt object and died instantly.

I left the next day for Mexico with Olga, where we spent two glorious months naked storytelling in the mountains. By the time we got back, the house had sold for over two million. I paid off

Adelle's gambling debts, which totalled almost a million dollars. Then I proposed to Olga, which she accepted, and promptly moved into her cozy Kitsilano apartment.

After going back to teach in the fall, and enjoying my first holiday season with my stunning fiancée, I had worked hard evenings and weekends on the first draft of my new book: *Death of a Dream: Why Students and Teachers Need to Fart More in Class*. I finished it at the end of January, and Olga was happily reading it through for me before I sent it to the publisher.

"Harry," said Olga, running up behind me. "Sorry. I didn't mean to leave you hanging like that."

I stopped and pulled Olga aside so we were right up against the lockers. "Listen, it doesn't matter—"

"No. You listen. This is my story, not yours."

"Actually, you're going to be my wife, so this is my story."

"Well, this is an ending for me, my ending, so will you shut up and listen!"

I stuck my beard out at her and pressed my lips closed so hard they went numb along the edges.

"Good," said Olga, looking up at me. "Rally and I had a long conversation this morning after you went to Jitters. He's finally got it through his thick organ that we are through. No more trying to woo me back. No more gifts. No more phone calls. And he's agreed," she paused, "to go to his lawyer's office to sign the papers this afternoon. It's over."

She smiled.

I couldn't smile. Not yet. I asked her, "But do you trust him?"

"Normally, I would say no, but in this case, I know he'll keep his word. We can set a date for the wedding and book Positano."

I looked at her suspiciously. "How can you be so sure?"

Olga whispered, "It's my story, my ending." She smiled and said with a loud, motherly tone, "Now, go get my coffee and hurry back so we catch part of the keynote."

"Yes, Ma'am," I said. "We don't want to miss Dr. So-and-so's big speech. But you have to tell me first."

"Tell you what?" said Olga, batting her eyelashes.

"The ending. How do you know Rally will sign the divorce papers?"

A mischievous glint appeared in her dark eyes. "He knows that I know a large, hairy storyteller who knows how to use a sledgehammer."

I almost told her the truth at that moment—all of it—but that was my story, my private ending, so, instead, I let it go, saying, "I never told you this, but I tossed my sledgehammer into False Creek the night my mother passed away."

She shrugged. "Rally doesn't know that, does he?"

I looked around. The hallway was thinning out as teachers made their way to the auditorium. "Let me get the coffees, and I'll hurry back to get you." I winked. "If I'm lucky, I'll get to see the real naked storyteller in person soon, very soon." I put my hand in my pocket and fingered the fifty-dollar chip from my big night at the comedy club. "I've got something special I want to give you tonight."

Olga rolled her eyes then kissed me on the cheek. "What have I started?" She pulled away but held onto my forearms. "Hurry back."

At the cream and sugar table, I received a swift, unwarranted jolt in the lower back which made me slop coffee on my turtleneck.

James, thin as ever, neatly dressed in black except for bright red sneakers, slapped me hard on the back, helping me spill even more coffee, on the table cloth, this time. "Back at the scene of the crime, eh?" he joked.

"Funny," I said, putting lids on my coffee and Olga's.

"So Beast's got a workshop this year."

"Yes, and it's full. But don't worry, we reserved a spot for you."

"Bah!" said James, pouring two coffees. "I'm skipping out. I just stopped by for the free coffee and to wish you luck. Philomena is in the car. We're going down to the casino for the weekend. That reminds me. You still owe me ten bucks."

"Do I?"

He nodded.

"Skipping out? That's pretty ballsy for a young buck like you," I said, pulling a folded-up ten-dollar bill out of my pocket and handing it to him.

James accepted it and said, "Can I ask you something?"

"Make it quick. I've got to help Olga set up."

James licked his lips. "I've seen what you've been doing with your students this year—can I be the first person to read your new book?"

I pretended to think about it for a moment, then blurted out, "Nope."

James's face fell. "Okay. I just thought maybe—"

"You can be the second."

He smiled. "Thanks, Beast." Then he raised his coffee to me and said, "To the naked storyteller."

"To the naked storyteller," I said, raising my cup.

We drank in silence, nodded at each other, then I watched my young friend hustle through the empty foyer and out through the glass doors.

During the break, after our successful naked storytelling workshop, I went out to my new car, a Fiat 500 Abarth, bright orange, and opened the hatchback. I lifted up the lid on the storage compartment in the trunk and touched the smooth wooden handle of my six-pound sledgehammer. I wouldn't be needing it now that Rally was going to sign the divorce papers. Maybe that would be a good idea for a novel, a murder mystery: *Who Killed Rally Kite?*

As I entered the foyer of the high school, I stopped just inside the doors to take off my trench coat. That's when I finally noticed the sign painted on the wall to the right of the doors which said in two-foot high, blue script: *Be the author of your own life.*

That evening, while Olga was reading my manuscript, I took my sledgehammer for a walk over the Granville Street Bridge and tossed it in.

ABOUT THE AUTHOR

LAURA MICHELLE THOMAS is an author with an opinion on just about everything she thinks is wrong with contemporary life in North America (which, in her opinion, is just about everything). Harry Tyke, the 52-year-old protagonist of *The Naked Storyteller*, is who Laura might be if she wasn't the author of her own life and had a beard. When she's not writing and telling her family to buzz off and let her work, she's runs a very busy website through which she fosters the development of young writers around the world through annual writing contests, young writers conferences and other inspirational stuff. With the assistance of her team of junior bloggers, editors and artists, Laura has the privilege of being publisher and senior editor of an international e-zine for young writers called *jaBlog!* To find out what book project Laura is working on now, please visit her website (www.laurathomascommunications.com) and click on "Novels by Laura Michelle Thomas."

CPSIA information can be obtained at www.ICGtesting.com
Printed in the USA
LVOW12s1611090914

403214LV00002B/244/P